They Always Come Back
Bailey Thomas

Bailey Thomas Books, LLC

Copyright © 2024 by Bailey Thomas

All rights reserved.

No portion of this book may be reproduced in any form without written permission from the publisher or author, except as permitted by U.S. copyright law.

You accept the love you think you deserve.

Contents

1. Viva Las Vegas — 1
2. Meet Cute — 7
3. Ethan Wiley — 17
4. The Pact — 27
5. Parental Control — 35
6. Game On — 39
7. Phone Home — 45
8. Dinner Date — 55
9. Trouble in Paradise — 61
10. Cooking up a Storm — 69
11. Party Foul — 75
12. Breakfast in Bed — 85
13. Change Is Inevitable — 93
14. Picture Perfect — 101
15. Team Bride — 107
16. Make a Wish — 113
17. The Bright Side — 121
18. Craving S'More — 129

19.	Daredevil	135
20.	Love at First Bite	145
21.	Battle Cry	153
22.	Terrible Twos	161
23.	Risky Appetite	167
24.	All Good Things Come to an End	173
25.	Opportunity Knocks	179
26.	Home Is Where the Exe Is	185
27.	Enough	191
28.	They Always Come Back	197

1
Viva Las Vegas

"They always come back." At least that's what my best friend Paige used to say when her cats Leo and Toby were nowhere to be found. According to her, they were adventurous explorers, getting a feel for their new environment, but as far as I could tell, they were just trying to escape the Las Vegas heat. They returned only once they'd found out that the desert was a lot more expansive than they originally thought. The scorching temperatures and brutal terrain were not for the faint of heart. I wouldn't have been surprised if they were plotting their ruthless feline getaway to California by now.

"Help me pick out an outfit," Paige urged as she held up two bikinis. "Red or black?"

"Red," I answered selfishly. Paige looked good in both, but I had planned on wearing a black swimsuit, and the last thing I wanted was to be compared to her.

She held up the red bathing suit to her body and started posing in the mirror as if she were being photographed for a fashion magazine. With her good looks and effortlessly toned body, I wouldn't be surprised if she was actually on the cover of one someday.

"All the boys are going to drool over me in this," she announced as she struck a few more poses.

I nodded in agreement, but wondered if there would be any male attention left over for me once they were done checking her out.

From the moment I met Paige Jensen, she had appeared confident in herself. Her light brown hair, hazel eyes, and bubbly personality left every man swooning over her and every girl jealous of her. Her freckles danced against her fair skin in the sun, and she had curves in just the right places. She had a glowing smile that could light up a room and a laugh that was dangerously contagious. Although she was of average height, her long legs made her appear taller.

Paige and I had been best friends since high school and even lived together during our senior year, and it didn't take long for me to notice the attention she commanded when she walked into a room. She had a severe caffeine addiction and an obsession with fashion, preferring to start her mornings with a vanilla latte while reading the latest style blog. The only thing she loved more than coffee and clothes were her two cats.

We were inseparable, but as much as we hung out, her overwhelming beauty and charm did not rub off on me. Paige and I could not have been more different. Her light features stood in contrast to my brunette hair and dark brown eyes. Her outgoing personality made my introverted energy stick out like a sore thumb. While Paige preferred to be the center of attention, I wanted to hide in the shadows. I couldn't have cared less about fancy caffeinated drinks, what was in style, or viral cat videos. I enjoyed quiet nights in my living room, cuddled up watching romantic comedies under a warm blanket that I'd bought from a thrift store. However, I think our differences made our friendship stronger. I don't think I could have asked for a better best friend.

Paige and I had attended East Tawas High School together, which wasn't surprising since it was the only high school in our town. Our graduating class consisted of roughly two hundred students, so although Paige and I didn't have that many classes together, our paths always seemed to cross.

I spent most of my days studying and tutoring math. Paige spent most of hers flirting with the latest hottie of the week. She failed our ninth-grade algebra exam on purpose so that she could get tutored by her newest crush, Hunter Stevens. When she realized that he was more interested in her brother than her, she dropped him. We got to know each other when I was assigned to be her new math tutor.

"Hi! I am Paige Jensen," she greeted me enthusiastically as she sat down at the table across from me.

From the moment she introduced herself, I knew she was different. She had a headstrong attitude and carefree spirit. Paige never paid attention to anyone's opinion of her, and she marched to the beat of her own drum. She was a force to be reckoned with, and I admired her ability to stand out in a crowd without getting lost in the noise.

"Avery Kline," I returned, trying—but failing—to match her energy. "So which algebra chapter are you struggling with?"

I loved being a math tutor, but sometimes getting my peers to actually open the textbook was the biggest challenge. They would rather have had me do their homework than learn anything. Once they figured out that I wasn't the type of tutor to help them cheat, they'd eventually let me teach them, but usually never returned for another session. Judging by the fact that Paige's math book still hadn't left the abyss of her backpack, I figured she would be one of those students.

"I'm actually not having a hard time with math," she admitted casually. "I just wanted an excuse to get to know Hunter Stevens, but that's over, so I figured I'd use being tutored as a way to make new friends." She must have taken my silence for an answer, because she continued. "You know he has a crush on my brother?"

This loud confession was met by a bunch of annoyed looks from those who were actually trying to study in the silence of the library. Paige didn't seem to notice or care about the irritated glances being sent her way.

"Well, is your brother hot?" I whispered sarcastically, in an effort to not further disturb those around me.

Paige shot me a menacing look, which was soon followed by boisterous laughter once she realized I was kidding. We spent the rest of the session giggling and talking about her brother's secret admirer, the newest fashion trends, and trending cat videos until we eventually got kicked out. After that day, Paige and I became best friends, and our math grades rose to the top of the class.

Paige was good at math, but I'd always had a special gift for the subject. Most would say it was because I was good with numbers, but I would argue that it was because math had been the most reliable thing in my life. During my sophomore year, my father won the lottery. He had an obvious gambling addiction that everyone quickly overlooked when, one Tuesday night, he used his last dime to buy a lottery ticket that ended up winning him $17 million. By that Friday, he and my mom had packed up to travel the world, while I was left behind in the care of my Aunt Joan. My mom was so grateful that her sister-in-law had stepped up, but I was convinced my father had slid her a few extra dollars to take over his parental duties. Finances weren't an issue anymore, and he couldn't let his only child get in the way of his new lifestyle.

Aunt Joan and I did not get along. She viewed kids as a burden, and therefore, did not have any of her own. She'd never married and preferred the company of crossword puzzles over humans. She wasn't thrilled to be my new guardian, but money was a powerful motivator. As soon as I turned eighteen, she kicked me out of her house, and I spent the rest of my senior year living with Paige, as she was the only other person whom I considered family that resided in the state of Michigan.

I occasionally received texts from my parents with photos from their latest venture, but that was the extent of our relationship. My dad periodically sent me a minor portion of the winnings, but I figured it was mostly because he wanted to ease the guilt he felt over being an absent father. At first, I was super grateful for the periodic stipends, as I used them to help pay for college. However, when my parents didn't even show up for my graduation or congratulate me via text, I realized the funds were truly just hush money. They were paying for my silence in regard to their sudden abandonment. I was still happy to have the money, but a relationship with my parents would have been far more valuable. I was twenty-two now, and I still hadn't seen them since the night they started their world travels.

"Avery Kline!" Paige shouted.

I must have zoned out, because she only ever used my full name when I was in trouble or lost in thought.

"Are you going to get ready or not?" She giggled as she threw her red bikini at me. "It's our first pool party in Vegas, and we have to be the hottest girls there."

I groaned as I removed myself from her bed and trudged over to my room. It was nice to finally have a reason to leave the apartment, but living in a new city was already stressful enough, and now I had to find the energy to socialize.

Paige and I had moved to Las Vegas from Michigan the week before. To her, this was a chance to party, escape the Midwest weather, and embark on a best friend adventure. Her reasoning was mostly correct. I couldn't deny that the thought of moving to such a lively place had excited me at first. A place nicknamed "Sin City" was not for the weak. The hot weather, endless pool parties, and exciting nightlife would have been enough to persuade anyone to give up the gloominess of Michigan, except for me.

If I could have spent the rest of my life in the small city of East Tawas, Michigan, I would have—in a heartbeat. I loved the friendly neighbors and serene nature, not to mention the second-to-none Detroit-style pizza. Michigan was my happy place. I had spent my entire twenty-two years of life there, but even that was not enough. I would have stayed there forever, but a boy had ruined it for me. Ethan Wiley was the cause of most of my latest breakdowns. He'd not only ruined my hometown, but all the memories that came along with it. I let my ex-boyfriend taint the very place that meant the most to me, and eventually I had no other choice but to leave.

I'd been staring into the mirror for fifteen minutes now. My hair was pulled back in a slick bun, accompanied by a light application of makeup and modest black bikini that I put on in an attempt to be the "hottest girl" at the pool party. However, I quickly realized that I was fighting for the title of "second hottest girl" when I walked into the kitchen and saw

Paige had ditched the original bikini option and decided to wear her black one instead.

"I wasn't really feeling the red," she explained when she saw the disappointment on my face. "But now we are twinning!"

She pulled me in for a hug, unaware that the defeated look on my face was not because she'd decided to go against my swimsuit suggestion, but because I realized that I would never look as good as Paige Jensen.

2

Meet Cute

When Paige and I decided to move across the country, we took apartment hunting very seriously. We probably went on ten tours before finally deciding on Exe Apartments on the southwest side of Vegas. It checked all of our boxes; spacious two-bedroom floor plan, view of the city, and within budget. However, the true selling point of the complex was the infamous parties. While touring the Exe, we were shown the deck, which featured two gorgeous pools, a hot tub, three grills, a lounge area with couches and chairs that were carefully maintained, and an elaborate pool bar. Our guide wasted no time in showing us the area and telling us about the amazing gatherings that the complex hosted every Saturday in the summers. We were in complete awe of the outdoor amenities, but the idea of the space being filled with people, music, and food was the most intriguing part. Paige and I signed on the spot.

    As we were leaving the leasing office, having just signed our life away for at least a year, a tall, muscular man with the kindest eyes held the door open for us as we exited. He gave Paige a slight nod, which left her blushing. She told me later she'd felt it was a sign that we had chosen the right place to live. However, I felt differently when we pulled away from the parking lot and passed a sign that said, "Home is where the Exe is." How fitting.

    After moving in and taking some time to adjust to our new home, the day had finally come when Paige and I would get to see if the main reason we'd signed our lease was actually worth it. We grabbed our bags and headed for the door, excited to experience our first Exe Apartments summer event. Paige's designer tote perfectly matched her summer sandals and sheer swimsuit cover. She looked picturesque from head to toe. I was still using an East Tawas High School backpack with the accompanying school-issued water bottle, but at least I was matching too. Paige assured me that there would be water at the party, but I didn't want to take any chances in the Vegas heat. In all honesty, I think she just wanted me to ditch the high school memorabilia, but I would have worn the matching hat as well if it hadn't been for my best friend's side job as the fashion police.

"Don't forget the key," Paige reminded as we walked out the door.

She never had her apartment key on her, claiming to be the more irresponsible one of us. Funnily enough, she somehow always remembered to remind me about it.

"Don't worry, I've got it," I responded as I locked the door behind us.

We navigated the twisting hallways toward the pool deck, fully unaware of what to expect. I was grateful we weren't too far from our destination, because every step we took made me want to turn around. Thankfully, we had opted for a unit on the ground floor so that Paige could let her cats explore, which put us on the same level as the pool. This worked in our favor since the number of people using the elevators was clearly more than they could handle. Even the hallways were packed to their limits. Paige and I had to squeeze our way through entire crowds of residents before we were even able to make it outside.

"Oh my, there are so many cute guys!" Paige exclaimed as we walked past a group of average-looking men.

I scanned the crowd and as much of the pool deck as I could see from our position in line, but nobody caught my eye, a typical letdown. I didn't consider myself picky, but I definitely didn't find as many guys attractive as Paige did. I considered my standards pretty reasonable, but so far only one guy had been able to steal my heart, and he was the reason why I'd had to leave Michigan.

"IDs," the guard demanded when Paige and I approached the entrance.

The pool area was enclosed by the surrounding apartment units, and the only way to access it was through a gate that was constantly guarded. The Exe had hired a security guard who was in charge of maintaining the safety and peace of the pool deck and its residents. It must have been some type of requirement to have a staff member on duty during operating hours, but they didn't seem to care that much considering that the young man they'd chosen appeared to have only been selected for his muscular body type. He didn't seem to have endured any real training. His uniform was a basic gray T-shirt that said "Security" on the back. He didn't carry any type of weapon, except for his bulging biceps, and his lack of scarring revealed that he hadn't been in any real combat. I found it odd that there was a security officer on duty and not a lifeguard, but I was sure his job description included rescuing helpless swimmers too.

He intently examined Paige's ID, which thankfully she'd remembered to bring, to ensure she was old enough to enter the 21+ event. I was grateful he didn't work for airport security, because he barely even peeked into her tote. She could have hidden a whole arsenal in there and he wouldn't have noticed. For both of our sakes, I decided I wouldn't be getting into the water anytime soon. I wasn't willing to find out if his CPR skills were as ineffective as his bag-searching skills.

Lucky for me, my thoughts must have been displayed across my forehead like a billboard sign, because when it was my turn to be searched, he stopped me.

"No outside alcohol," he reprimanded, pointing at my water bottle.

"Oh, don't worry, she doesn't drink," Paige interrupted. Although he'd let her into the pool area, she was staying close by until I was able to enter with her.

"You live in Vegas, and you don't drink?" He unscrewed my water bottle to smell the liquid inside.

"You don't have to drink to live in Vegas," I replied, with an obvious attitude.

The security guard looked at me inquisitively and handed me back my water. He examined me with a great deal of curiosity, and I returned the same look with a load of sass.

"You can at least close it next time," I muttered sharply as I walked past him. If he was going to give me a hard time for bringing water to a pool in the middle of July, then he could at least do me the favor of screwing the cap back on. The friendly culture of the Midwest must not have made its way to Nevada yet.

Paige grabbed my arm and dragged me toward the last two available pool chairs. We laid our stuff out to claim the area and prepared ourselves for our first pool party. I pulled out my romance novel and began to read while Paige laid out in the sun to tan and scan the area for cute guys to flirt with. It wasn't surprising that I was the only one there with a book in their hand, but the last thing I wanted to do was listen to the electronic dance music that was blaring through the speakers or fraternize with ugly-looking dudes.

While nose-deep in my novel, I paused every couple of lines to peer at the security guard as he shuffled through other residents' belongings. It was nice to know that I wasn't the only one he was stopping, but I couldn't help but notice that when these girls were being searched, they smiled a little sweeter, laughed a little louder, and hiked their bikini bottoms up just a little higher. A few of them even carried on a short conversation with the guard before they walked in. He was evidently popular among the females, but watching him soak up all of the attention was a complete turnoff. Women were flaunting their bikini bodies at him, and he was not turning them down. He must've been desperate.

"I see you've noticed Kyle," an unfamiliar voice said to me.

"Who is Kyle?" I responded, even though it didn't take a rocket scientist to figure out who this girl was talking about. I guess I had been staring a little too hard at him for her not to notice. I didn't think I'd been watching him that intently, but I also couldn't remember the last time I had turned a page in my book.

The strange girl took a seat next to me, and I was able to get a better look at her short stature and fiery red hair. I recognized her as one of the women who had been flaunting themselves to him.

"The pool security guard," she explained. "He is so hot, but he doesn't date residents."

The conversation piqued Paige's interest, and she sat up and removed her sunglasses to get a better look at him. "He is kinda hot," she proclaimed, after eyeing him up and down a few times.

"He's new this year," the unfamiliar girl informed us. "He only started a couple of months ago, but everyone already loves him."

"Well, I don't," I uttered sharply. "He had the audacity to give me a hard time about not drinking." I fired a nasty look in his direction, even though he was too far away to notice.

"You live in Vegas, and you don't drink?" the girl asked in shock, but at this point it just sounded like a broken record. She must have picked up on the fact that I'd already heard that line, because she quickly explained herself. "Sorry," she said, "I'm just not used to that, but that's great! I wish I didn't drink either."

Another line I had heard plenty of times before.

"I am Hannah, by the way." She shook hands with Paige and me.

"Paige Jensen."

"Avery," I responded.

"Nice to meet you both," Hannah exclaimed. "I live on the third floor with my cat, Tubs."

This excited Paige, and she and Hannah ended up having their own side conversation about the personalities of their cats. Although slightly annoying, it gave me time to focus my attention back on Kyle. I made a mental note to get a better look at him when we decided to leave, since I'd been too flustered to notice him the first time and now I was too far away to see any of his features clearly. I could only tell that he had sandy blonde hair and a tall, athletic build. From what I could decipher, he was actually kinda cute, but I wasn't interested in dating someone who thrived on female attention.

After a few hours of tanning, swimming, and dancing with our new friend Hannah, Paige and I returned back to our apartment, grateful again that we didn't have to use the crammed elevators. We unpacked our bags and raced to our showers to wash away the remnants of the pool party.

Once we were clean, we shared our thoughts on the day over takeout Chinese food and a classic romantic comedy. Although slightly bummed that she hadn't gotten to flirt with as many guys as she'd hoped, Paige considered the party to be a success since we got to meet Hannah.

"You know her cat, Tubs, has the same birthday as my second cousin?" she said.

I nodded and pretended to be interested as she continued to go on and on about their conversation, which had revolved solely around their cats. While she rambled, all I could think about was how I'd forgotten to get another good look at Kyle before we left.

"Tubs also eats the same brand of cat food that Toby and Leo do!" Paige cried out excitedly.

Fortunately, I was saved from listening to any more when Paige's phone rang for her weekly Saturday-night catch-up with her mom. Sometimes I wished I had a parent who would call me every week, so that I could tell them about my day, but I was happy for Paige and smiled as she excitedly ran off to her room for some privacy. Conversations with her mother usually lasted over an hour, so I decided to take one of my romance novels and head back to the pool for some peaceful reading. For obvious reasons, I hadn't made much progress in my book earlier, so I figured now would be the perfect opportunity to make up for lost time.

I quietly exited our apartment and headed straight for the pool deck. To my surprise, Kyle was still on duty. However, not to my surprise, he was on the receiving end of another girl trying to flirt with him. I rolled my eyes and scoffed at her lame attempt to impress him. Kyle looked at me at the exact moment that disgust flooded my face. I instantly wanted to turn around and pretend that I'd never even been in the area, but I was in too deep. Instead, I flashed a gentle smile, walked briskly past them to the nearest pool chair, and opened my book. I was too nervous to find another reading spot, so I'd opted for the first empty seat I saw. It was positioned close enough to Kyle and his latest suitor that I could hear every word of their conversation.

"So what time are you off?" The girl seductively twirled her long blonde hair.

"Eleven," he answered nonchalantly.

Even from my reading spot, I could hear the desperation in her voice.

"Do you want to hang out after your shift?" she asked impatiently. "You can come to my place."

I couldn't help but laugh to myself hearing this woman completely throw herself at him. She wasn't even his type. I may not have known his type, or if he even had one, but whatever it was, it wasn't her. Her flushed face resembled her hot-pink jacket and matching leggings. She was clearly motivated by style over comfort, considering it was over ninety degrees outside.

"I can't," Kyle explained. "I have another shift tomorrow morning."

The girl grumbled and stormed off, seeming annoyed and disappointed that Kyle hadn't taken the bait. She was clearly aware of his reputation for not getting himself involved with people who lived at the Exe, but had decided to give it a try anyway. I watched her hot-pink outfit disappear out of sight.

I returned to my book, but couldn't focus, as I kept looking up every couple of minutes or so to watch Kyle. He spent the rest of his shift organizing lounge chairs, cleaning the pool bar, and throwing away trash left over from the party. It was the kind of lackluster job that a normal person would complain about, but Kyle seemed to enjoy his responsibilities. As I watched him discard the last stray can, we made brief eye contact. I quickly looked away and went on to act as though I was engrossed in my book. Admittedly, I hadn't read a single word in the last twenty minutes. I glanced up again, relieved that he had resumed his normal duties. I curiously watched him as he continued to move around a few more lounge chairs. He was still too far away for me to fully make out his physical features, but his beautiful smile seemed to surpass any distance.

Kyle was heading back to his usual position at the entrance when my heart stopped. He'd walked right past the gate and was headed straight in my direction. I wanted to return to the safety of my book, but my eyes were already locked with his. It would be way too obvious if I looked away now. My breath became short, and the world around me started to disappear as he got closer. For a moment, I could have sworn we were the only two people out on the pool deck—or the only two people in the world.

My trance was suddenly broken when his six-foot-four athletic frame towered over me as I sat in the comfort of the lounge chair. His tan complexion complemented his dirty-blonde hair, and his uniform hugged his chest and biceps in all the right places. He had a large snake tattoo that took up most of his left forearm. It was a frightening creature that had a devilish look in its eyes. An unusual marking for a guy that seemed anything but evil. My eyes were quickly redirected from the tattoo toward the veins in his arms, which were bulging under his skin. His eyes were a perfect shade of golden brown and could have hypnotized any soul daring enough to get lost in them, and his lips were almost too tempting to even look at.

"I'm sorry to ask this," he slowly began, "but were you staring at me?"

His question snapped me back to reality, and I remembered that I would have to somehow formulate a response to this handsome man. Since my heart wasn't helping me think straight, my brain decided to take over and answer with a less than ideal reply.

"I actually was staring at you," I casually admitted, "but only because you were staring at me."

I cringed at my own response. If it had been socially acceptable to run away in the middle of a conversation, I would've been headed for my apartment by now, but unfortunately that probably would've made matters worse—if that were even possible.

"Well, I couldn't help myself." His eyes meticulously scanned every inch of me. "I liked what I saw."

This simple compliment sent a warm rush through my entire body. I had to turn away from him slightly to hide my cheeks, which were radiating a shade of bright red.

"I'm Kyle, by the way." He stuck out his hand for me to shake. "Kyle Kingsley."

"Avery Kline," I said. I shook his obnoxiously large hand and couldn't help but wonder what other parts of him were unusually large.

"I remember you from earlier today," he announced. "You're the girl that lives in Vegas but doesn't drink." He gave a small chuckle. "Are you also allergic to the sun and have a crippling fear of casinos? Because if that's the case, then I have some really bad news for you."

I let out a quiet giggle, shocked by how easy it was for him to make me laugh. It had taken Kyle less than a minute, while other guys couldn't even get me to smile.

"I'm not afraid of casinos," I proudly asserted, "but I am a little freaked out by that snake tattoo you have."

I pointed to his arm, where the serpent lived, but quickly retracted my finger. For some reason, I had an irrational fear of it suddenly coming to life and inserting its venom into my fingertip.

"Oh, don't worry about him," Kyle said gently. "He doesn't bite."

I was still seated in the lounge chair, so he lowered himself to my height and whispered into my ear, "He only chokes."

He gave me a sly wink and dismissed himself back to the gate. I watched him walk away, too stunned by his response to react. There was something about him that intrigued me. I wanted to know more, but at the same time, I was afraid of what I might find.

I'd once been told that you should never wound a snake, that if you ever came across one, you should kill it, because it would always find a way to bite you in the end. I thought I might've found my snake, but I refused to kill him.

3
Ethan Wiley

I woke up earlier than usual the next morning. The sunlight was shining through my windows, invading every crevice of my bedroom, though there was not much to invade as most of my stuff was still in boxes. I preferred minimalist decor anyway, so once I was able to finally muster up the energy to officially unpack, my room would still look mostly bare.

I stared down at my heaving chest and the sweat stains that soaked the oversized T-shirt that I'd designated my pajama shirt. Even after a week of living in Vegas, I still sometimes woke up in a panic, not knowing where I was, until I eventually realized that it wasn't just a dream that my best friend and I had decided to move across the country to a new city. It was the most courageous thing I had ever done in my life, and I was happy that I'd gotten to do it with my best friend. One day I would get used to the fact that I'd basically been forced to leave my old life behind because of my narcissistic ex, but for now I would continue to suffer through my mini morning panic attacks.

It was only eight when I awoke on Sunday morning, and the pool didn't open until ten, but the thought of seeing Kyle again was enough to get me out of bed. Last night, I couldn't help but replay every moment with him until I fell asleep. There was something different about him, and I was determined to figure him out.

I had already picked out the next bikini I wanted to wear. It was a bright-yellow high-waisted two-piece that was less modest than the black one I had worn yesterday, but still more fabric than all of Paige's swimsuits combined. I styled my hair into two perfect French braids and applied just the right amount of makeup—not so little that someone might question if I was wearing any, but just enough to be noticeable. I usually refrained from trying to put in any effort into looking cute because I could never compete with Paige. It was easier to just blend in than try to match her beauty, but this morning I was feeling extra confident.

I made my way to the kitchen and found Paige sitting at the dining table. "You're up early," she said as she glanced up from her phone, taking a brief break from reading the latest fashion blog to sip her vanilla latte.

I seemed to have erred too much on the side of "not noticeable" when I did my makeup, since my own best friend couldn't tell that I was wearing any.

"Couldn't sleep," I half-heartedly lied. Of course I hadn't slept much last night, but it had nothing to do with the Vegas sun and everything to do with the mysterious security guard.

I grabbed a protein bar, took a seat across from Paige, and watched Toby and Leo wrestle on the couch. I decided not to tell her about the little interaction I'd had with Kyle, at least not right away. I wasn't in the mood to answer any questions about a situation I hadn't even wrapped my own head around yet, and I definitely didn't want to answer her questions if nothing came from it. I made the conscious decision to tell her about Kyle if and when there was something worth telling.

"Do you want to go to the mall with Hannah and me today?" Paige asked after slurping down the rest of her coffee.

I was really looking forward to heading to the pool deck as soon as it opened. However, I was running out of cute swimwear options. After the yellow suit that I had planned on wearing today, I wouldn't have many choices left except for ones that only a grandma would wear. Besides, I didn't need to spend the entire day at the pool.

"Of course," I responded cheerfully.

"Great. She will be here in an hour," Page relayed, excusing herself from the kitchen table and heading to her bedroom to get dressed for our mall adventure. "Hannah also mentioned going up to the pool deck later today. She said something about five-dollar appetizers at the bar on Sundays."

"Sounds good to me," I replied as I scarfed down my protein bar.

My mission to get to know Kyle better would have to wait a few more hours.

"That looks so cute on you!" Hannah screeched as Paige walked out of the fitting room to show off the new swimsuit she was trying on.

"You look stunning!" I announced in an effort to further boost my friend's already high self-esteem.

"Thank you!"

Paige checked herself out in the mirror. She'd chosen a bright-blue swimsuit with neon-green stripes that accentuated her curves. With the amount of time she spent browsing fashion magazines, I knew she understood which styles and patterns were trending, so I ended up choosing a bright bikini of my own.

"Okay, Hannah, you're next!" Paige announced as she walked away from the mirror.

She wandered over to the seat next to me as Hannah took her spot in the fitting room. Her hazel eyes glistened in the artificial lighting as she scooted closer to me.

"Moving here was the best decision ever," Paige proclaimed as she leaned over and gave me a hug.

"Best decision ever," I confirmed as I wrapped my arms around her. "I can't believe we actually did it."

She smiled and laughed in agreement. I don't think she realized how grateful I was to have her by my side or how grateful I was to be thousands of miles away from my ex. When I first brought up the idea of moving away, Paige had been hesitant. She loved East Tawas as much as I did, and she couldn't understand why I would suggest leaving.

After weeks of me showing her pool party videos, downplaying the amenities Michigan had to offer, and describing how much this move would strengthen our friendship, she'd agreed. I never told her that the main reason I wanted to leave the place where we'd created our fondest memories was to escape my ex-boyfriend, Ethan Wiley, but I was sure she could probably guess.

Ethan and I had met on our first day at Tawas Michigan University. Even as a freshman stepping foot onto campus for the first time, he was well-known. He'd been a high school football star whose reputation had swept the nation when he announced that he was taking his talents to TMU. Most people had assumed he would commit to a larger university since he was ranked as the number two quarterback in the country, but his mom had fallen severely ill during his junior year, which he pointed to as the reason that he wanted to play football near his hometown.

When Ethan walked into my chemistry class, I was amused by his tall and heroic stature. He walked as if the world revolved around him, and at that point in time, I wouldn't have been surprised if it had. He always strutted around campus in TMU football attire, his head held high. He was liked by everyone, especially the girls. In hindsight, I could see that most of his college friendships had been one-sided relationships he'd used to gain an advantage, but back then, nobody cared. They just wanted to be involved in his life in any way that they could.

While reviewing the Introduction to Chemistry syllabus, Ethan had sat down in the empty chair next to me and immediately took out his phone. He didn't even take a second to take in his surroundings or, more importantly, look at who he was sitting next to. I could have grown two heads, and he wouldn't have known. While he was too preoccupied with scrolling through social media to even care about the world around him, I couldn't help but notice that he had the most beautiful chocolate-brown curls. They danced with every slight movement he made and sat perfectly above his jawline. His green eyes were piercing but friendly, and his lips were the perfect shade of pink. I bet myself they tasted like fresh red strawberries.

My daydreaming was abruptly interrupted by the sound of Professor Townes starting the lecture, a huge disappointment to all the students who'd thought that the first day would just consist of reviewing the syllabus.

"I hope you all have had a chance to meet the person sitting next to you," the professor announced, "because they will be your chemistry partner for the semester."

This was met with a quiet uproar of grumbles. If we had known that we would be working with the person beside us, we would have scouted the room for the smartest kid in the class instead of sitting by our friends—or in my case, hot strangers.

"Please take the last few minutes to discuss how you will tackle the final project due at the end of the semester," Professor Townes noted.

The class groaned even louder.

I slowly turned toward Ethan, careful not to show how excited I was to be paired with TMU's football star. However, my enthusiasm went undetected as I discovered that he still hadn't even looked up from his phone.

"Looks like we are going to be chemistry partners," I explained, still trying to hide my smile, even though it was pointless.

"I'm sorry, beautiful," he started after glancing up. He shuffled around a bit and gathered his stuff before he continued, "But I am going to be missing a lot of class this semester because I have a championship to win."

I gazed at him, speechless. I couldn't decide whether I was mad that he was trying to pin this project on me or flattered that the star quarterback had called me beautiful.

"I'll try to help you as much as I can, but you are probably going to end up doing most of the project yourself," he explained.

I stared at him, dumbfounded. I appreciated his honesty, but I couldn't believe I'd been paired with a guy who was planning on barely helping me with the assignment. Before I could gather my thoughts to respond, he'd stood up to leave.

"You can come over tonight so we can discuss which parts of the project we will be doing," he remarked as he pushed in his chair. "I live in Wayside Dorms, room 522, on the south side of campus. See you at seven."

Ethan left the class despite not being dismissed. Professor Townes noticed, but said nothing. Perhaps he'd decided that he didn't want to become public enemy number one to the man that was going to lead the university to a championship.

Soon after, the bell rang, and I immediately headed to find Paige to tell her about my interesting encounter with the school's star quarterback.

I knocked on Ethan's door at exactly seven. I'd actually arrived at Wayside Dorms at six forty-five, but I couldn't decide if coming too early would look overeager, or if showing up too late would look disrespectful, so I opted for knocking on his door right on time.

"It's open!" I heard a voice yell. It did not sound like it belonged to Ethan. I double-checked the number just in case I'd shown up to the wrong room, but the golden numbers "522" were staring back at me, confirming that I was in the right place.

I opened the door hesitantly to find two large men, presumably Ethan's teammates, on a couch playing video games.

"He's the first door on your left," the larger one yelled without even looking at me.

It must have been a normal occurrence for 522 to have strange women over, since the guys didn't seem surprised to have a random girl walk through their door. I shuffled my way over to Ethan's room and gently knocked, nervous about what I was going to see on the other side.

"Come in!" shouted a voice that I recognized as Ethan's.

I slowly opened the door to find him watching TV in his typical TMU attire. I took a quick glance at my surroundings and was surprised by how clean everything was. I could tell his bed was made despite him currently lying on it. His closet door was open, and I could see that his clothes were organized by color. Oddly enough, his room even smelled like roses. Maybe Ethan wasn't as disorganized as he appeared, or maybe there had been another girl in here right before me.

"I like your room," I complimented, trying to break the silence and shift my thoughts away from what he and the potential mystery girl had been doing prior to my arrival.

"Thank you," he replied proudly.

I tried to keep my breathing as calm and as steady as possible and not allow myself to think about the fact that I was alone with Ethan Wiley. However, I was going to break character soon if he didn't stop looking at me with those gorgeous green eyes while wearing a T-shirt that was a size too small.

"I don't think I ever got your name," he said as he gently patted the empty spot on the bed next to him, insinuating that I should stop standing in the middle of the room and join him.

I hesitantly made my way toward him. I stood close enough to see all of his beautiful features in the glow of the television, but refused to let myself climb into bed with him.

"Avery Kline," I nervously uttered.

"Avery Kline," he repeated seductively. My name sounded so much better coming from his mouth. I wished he would say it more often.

"Once I finish this movie, we can start discussing our chemistry project, okay?" He clicked the remote to show me there were only fifteen minutes left. I nodded and continued to maintain a safe distance from him.

"Want some something to eat?" Ethan was already handing me a bowl of buttery popcorn and extended a second offer to accompany him in his bed so that we could more comfortably watch the last fifteen minutes of what seemed to be a WWII documentary. I grabbed a handful, but insisted on standing.

A few hours later, I returned to my dorm room without any progress having been made on our chemistry project. I was frustrated with my uncooperative partner, but at least I had been able to confirm that his lips did indeed taste like fresh red strawberries.

Ethan and I went on to date throughout college. I supported him through his entire football career and continued to "help" him with his academic work. By the start of his senior season, he had already brought TMU two championships and had professional scouts attending his practices. Ethan was on top of the world, and our relationship couldn't have been any stronger—until the first conference game of his last season. He tore his ACL and MCL in both knees and suffered a minor concussion. The guilty player was ejected, but Ethan's collegiate football career and dreams of playing professionally were over.

After more than a year of constant rest and rehabilitation, the pain from Ethan's injuries had subsided, but the relationship he had with his physical therapist had not. I came home early from work one night and found them cuddled up on the living room sofa that Ethan and I had fought over. When we'd initially moved in together junior year, I'd begged him to get rid of the couch, which he had owned since the beginning of freshman year. It still had stains on it and smelled like the bathroom of a frat house. Needless to say, it turned out to be the least of our worries.

After Ethan's career-ending injuries, our relationship was never the same. Football had been the one thing that bonded us together. I'd spent more time in the stands at TMU than at my own apartment. Ethan never got over the potential of what his future could have been, and he took his frustrations out on me. I had once been the girl he couldn't live without, but over time became the girl who continuously reminded him of what could have been. We constantly argued, and every day one of us threatened to end the relationship.

I knew I deserved better than a guy who laid around the apartment all day, barely contributed financially, and verbally abused me. But that's the thing about relationships; you don't realize that you have completely lost yourself in the never-ending battle of fighting against each other and fighting for each other until you are already in too deep. I guess it took me finding him sneaking around with his physical therapist to finally let that relationship go.

I was having a mini pity party for myself over the memories of my past relationship when Hannah exited the fitting room to strut around in the new bikini that she picked out. It was a slightly more modest style that resembled the one I had worn yesterday.

"Do you think Kyle will notice me in this?" she innocently asked as she stared at herself in the mirror.

Pity party over.

4
The Pact

Hannah, Paige, and I were finally making our way toward the pool in our new bikinis after spending most of the afternoon at the mall. My closet was satisfied with my most recent purchase, but my bank account would have begged to differ. Although my job as a social media manager for a modeling agency didn't pay that well, it had been nice to treat myself for once. Besides, my father sent me a check once a month that more than covered my bills. Even though I would have traded all the money he gave me for some quality father-daughter bonding time, I wasn't complaining about the additional funds. In his eyes, the checks must have been a sign of being a good father, but money didn't solve everything.

After graduating TMU with a degree in mathematics, I interned at a few financial institutions, but quickly learned that my love for math didn't extend beyond the classroom. Paige's mom graciously landed me an interview with Ace Modeling Agency, which was located in New York City. The only remote position available had been managing their social media accounts, so I reluctantly took on that role. I usually spent my workdays scrolling through the internet, gathering insights that my bosses used in strategic planning meetings, or answering aspiring models' inquiries, which seemed to always fill the inbox. My job seemed pretty on paper, but usually left me banging my head against the wall by the time five o'clock hit. If it were up to me, I would have quit after the first week, because staring at models on social media all day really puts a dent in your confidence, but I knew Paige's mom had pulled a lot of strings to get me this role, and I didn't want to disappoint her.

My position would have been better suited for a girl more like Paige—into fashion, always on social media, up to date on the latest trends—but she enjoyed spending her days as a nanny. She loved kids and they loved her. Unlike Paige, I could never have spent my afternoons watching other people's children. I could barely take care of myself, so being in charge of tiny humans would not have worked out well for either party. Although I had no interest in trading jobs with Paige in the near future, I did get a little envious during the times when the family that she worked for would plan extravagant vacations and fully pay for her to attend.

She always claimed that she was in it for the kids and not the lavish lifestyle, but she couldn't deny that getting paid to travel around the world was an amazing bonus. Nannies must also be in high demand in Nevada, because it hadn't taken her long to find a family in Vegas in need of childcare. I couldn't imagine the kinds of trips she would go on with them. They had more money than they knew what to do with and were always looking for a chance to escape the fast-paced life that the city had to offer. I missed my best friend when she was out being the world's best caretaker, but often, it gave me a chance to enjoy some time to myself.

As the three of us continued to navigate the apartment hallways on our way toward the pool deck, we received gawking stares as we walked past the other residents. We strutted down the corridors confidently, showing off our newest bikinis as if we were walking down a runway at a fashion show. While Paige and I had opted for bright-colored suits with fun patterns, which were apparently trending, Hannah had chosen a plain black swimsuit.

Although she'd decided on something simple, Hannah's shopping tendencies were anything but basic. She'd had to try on every single article of clothing that caught her attention, even if she had no intentions of buying it. We went into each store with the goal of only spending a few minutes browsing around, but ended up shopping for at least twenty minutes. She'd never failed to remind Paige and me that redheads couldn't wear red and that gray washed out her freckles. Paige was a good sport about it and gave constructive feedback on all of the clothes that Hannah tried on. However, if she hadn't been there, I would have considered dragging Hannah out of the mall after the bikini store. It wouldn't have been the worst thing in the world, because even after our three-hour shopping excursion, she'd ended up walking out with only the black bikini.

"Which appetizers are you going to get?" Hannah asked hungrily. "They are half-off on Sundays."

"I don't know, but I'm starving," Paige remarked. "What are you going to get, Avery?"

I had only eaten a mall pretzel in the past few hours, and my stomach was growling. "Probably the entire menu."

My comment was met with animated laughter from Hannah and Paige, but I don't think they knew I wasn't entirely joking.

After further conversation about all of the food that we were going to devour, we finally arrived at our destination. Hannah was the first one to walk through the doors to the pool deck, with Paige and I following close behind. We eventually made our way toward the gate, and standing there in his security uniform was none other than Kyle Kingsley.

My heart began racing as we walked toward him. His gorgeous blonde hair and muscular body looked even better in the prime lighting of the summer sun. The snake tattoo was still staring at me, but it looked less sinister during the day.

"I have to check your bags, ladies," he reminded us as we approached the gate, already opening our totes since we knew the drill by now.

After he'd done a less-than-average job looking through Hannah's and Paige's items, I walked up to him, holding open my bag with the only confidence I had left after his stoic presence had melted the rest of it away.

"Don't worry, Avery," he said with a smirk. "I don't need to check your bag."

He winked at me as he opened up the gate for us. It sent chills through my entire spine. My face blushed a shade of red that Hannah would never be caught wearing, and my knees became so weak that I had to try to remember how to walk.

"How does he know your name?" Paige inquired innocently as we passed him.

"He checked our IDs yesterday, remember?" I answered, thankfully remembering this detail at the last minute.

"Yeah, but why does he remember your name?" Hannah asked.

I tried to think of another excuse, but couldn't come up with anything useful. "Maybe he has a sister with the same name?" I responded, proudly aware that the likelihood of Kyle having a sister named Avery was very low.

"Do you guys want to order some appetizers?" I asked in attempt to change the subject.

"I'll have the chips and salsa!" Paige and Hannah excitedly shouted in unison.

"I think I'll do the same," I agreed.

We all headed in the direction of the bar, but I briefly looked over my shoulder to get one more glance at Kyle. He was busy checking in other residents, but managed to send another giant wink in my direction. My stomach filled with butterflies as I giddily skipped the rest of the way to the bar.

Paige and Hannah decided to return to their apartments after spending just thirty minutes at the pool and only finishing half of their appetizers. Paige wanted to return to her cats since she hadn't been home for the majority of the day, and Hannah wanted to sleep away the exhaustion from the stressful shopping trip. Paige and I arguably needed the rest more than she did, but we didn't say anything when she gingerly made her way back to her room. I chose to stay at the pool, as the alone time gave me the perfect opportunity to talk to Kyle.

I hadn't been surprised when Paige made the decision to go back to the apartment to hang out with her cats. Ever since she'd rescued Toby and Leo from the dumpster behind our high school, she'd considered them family. One day, Paige accidentally threw her retainer away during lunch, so as her best friend, I'd helped her dig through the school dumpster in an attempt to find it. Her mom constantly reminded her to take care of it, so she was afraid of telling her the truth about losing it. After an hour of rummaging through cafeteria garbage, we found two kittens gnawing on the retainer. Ever since, those cats had been the center of Paige's entire life.

As I finished the last of my chips and salsa, I watched Kyle and waited for there to be a break in his conversations before walking over to him. It took longer than I'd anticipated, because there always seemed to be a girl nearby who wanted his attention. I patiently waited as woman after woman approached him, each in their own attempt to be the one to steal his heart. After what seemed like an eternity, I eventually made my way over.

"Hey, Kyle," I excitedly greeted him.

"Hi, Avery," he returned, with an equal amount of enthusiasm.

"I've been trying to talk to you all day, but so many girls keep coming up to you," I blurted out, getting right to the point. I could have led with some more small talk, but Kyle seemed like the type of guy who liked things to be direct, and I wanted to say as much as possible before the next girl came to interrupt us.

"I know, I'm sorry," he said. "I've told all of them several times that I don't date residents, but they still insist on flirting with me."

My heart sank at the idea of him still sticking to his irrational rule, but rules were meant to be broken, right?

"Why don't you date residents?" I asked, maybe a little too eagerly.

Kyle briefly checked his surroundings. "The previous security guard that worked here went to help a girl who locked herself out of her unit," he continued. "It was all a trick to get him to come over to her apartment, and when he rejected her, she lied and told the apartment manager that they had been romantically involved. He was fired right on the spot." Kyle paused as if to take a moment of silence for the prior employee. "I actually like my job and would love to keep it until the pool closes in September."

He continued to explain the details of the story and occasionally paused to let me ask some of my own questions regarding the whole situation. We ended up talking for hours, until Kyle finally realized that half of his shift was over and no girl had interrupted us except to notify him that there was glass in the pool.

"Wow, can you stay with me every shift?" he asked. "I haven't had this much peace since I started."

"The other girls probably think that you're interested in me," I responded playfully. "They gave up on trying to flirt with you. I'm your resident repellent."

I laughed, but he didn't even crack a smile. Instead, he leaned in closer to me to show that he didn't want anyone else to hear what he was about to say.

"I'll make a pact with you," he whispered intently. "You agree to hang out with me during my shifts so that the other girls continue to leave me alone."

"And what do I get out of this pact?" I asked quizzically, even though I was already jumping at the idea of spending time with Kyle every weekend.

He leaned in even closer, and I could feel his breath on my lips. It took every ounce of restraint I had to fight the urge to kiss him. I wasn't exactly sold on the idea yet, but his golden-brown eyes were tempting me to look at them in an effort to seduce me into accepting any deal he proposed.

"You get to talk to me, of course," he said flirtatiously.

I wasn't the smartest person in the world, but I quickly realized that this agreement was severely one-sided. However, he already had me in a dangerous trance that not even the most disciplined person in the world would have been able to resist.

I reached out to shake his large hand. "I accept," I announced firmly.

5

Parental Control

I closed my laptop, signaling the end of the workday. After completing my fair share of researching social media trends within the male modeling industry, it was safe to say that I was officially an expert in counting abs. I had seen more biceps than I was willing to admit, and I could recreate the top five poses they all seemed to cycle through. It was a task that most would not complain about, but I was becoming numb to the male figure and yearned for the day when I would actually have the confidence to let Paige's mom know that the job wasn't for me.

Paige was sleeping over at the Thompsons', the family that she had been a nanny for since we moved to Vegas, so it was going to be a quiet night. I figured I could spend it binge-watching romantic movies and plotting how to get Kyle's number. It was only Wednesday, but it felt as though it had been an eternity since I'd last seen him. He only worked Fridays, Saturdays, and Sundays, so there were long gaps between opportunities to see him. Maybe if I was able to text him throughout the week, time would go by faster. So far, the only plan I could think of was just asking him directly.

I was in the middle of plotting Operation: Get Kyle's Number when I was interrupted by the vibration of my phone. Paige must have left something at the apartment and want me to bring it to her. She seemed to forget her charger every time she went somewhere for a long period of time, but the Thompsons' house was only two miles away, so it wasn't that much of a hassle. To my surprise, the word "Mom" popped up on the screen, accompanied by a text.

Just left Tokyo!

The message also contained a picture of a busy airport. I barely looked at it before deciding to move on with my night. I usually got these types of texts every month. They were mostly just check-ins to make sure I was still alive as opposed to messages from a loving mother who actually wanted to genuinely connect with her daughter and update her about her whereabouts. I wasn't sure how long seventeen million lasted, but it'd been about six years since my father won the lottery, and they were still traveling the world, which meant it has been about six years since I had last seen them.

After finishing my fourth movie, I realized how bored I was without Paige. I even contemplated finally unpacking the boxes in my room, but I quickly came to my senses. I wasn't that desperate. I would have invited Hannah over had she not already made plans with her other friends. Since moving to Vegas, I hadn't put much effort into meeting other people. I had Paige, and that was really all I needed. She had always been a loyal friend to me, and I didn't see the need to make any others. They would never be on the same level as her, and would probably end up disappointing me in the end anyway.

Paige, on the other hand, was a social butterfly. She had people outside our friendship she would occasionally hang out with or talk on the phone to. It was her mission to make as many friends as possible, which meant she always was talking to someone new. Her social life was a lot more active than mine.

During the fifth and final romantic comedy that I had committed myself to watching, Toby and Leo decided that the spot on the couch next to me would be their next playground. I didn't pay them much attention at first, but the constant scratching and cat hair flying around was starting to irritate me. I got up and grabbed a handful of their treats. Paige usually reserved them for special occasions, but this was an emergency. Toby and Leo recognized the sound of the bag being rummaged through and immediately paused their intense brawl to follow the smell in anticipation of a delicious snack. I quickly walked over to Paige's room, opened the door, and threw a handful of treats on her bed. The cats sprinted toward the feast, almost tripping me in the process. As soon as they were both distracted, I closed the door behind them. I didn't intend to hold Toby and Leo captive, but their feline antics were disturbing my peace.

After the movie, I spent the rest of my night lying in bed, scrolling through social media. I figured I'd use my internet skills to lurk on the very person who was in charge of protecting the safety of Exe residents at the pool. We would be spending a lot of time together because of our pact, so it only made sense to see what I could find about Kyle.

He wasn't hard to track down, because his social media handle was literally his first and last name. What a simple man. Unfortunately, his account had limited photos for me to examine. There were only two—one of his car and another of him and some friends at a nightclub. Neither offered much insight into his life. I clicked on the images to see who was liking and commenting on his page. They were mostly his guy friends or fake accounts. The attention he got from girls in real life must not have reached his social media yet.

I made my way toward the list of people he was following. There were a couple of residents that I recognized from the apartment complex, but most were models who didn't even follow him back, and one account belonged to my new friend, Hannah Livingston. Her page was full of pictures of her family and tropical getaways with her friends.

Without hesitation, I returned to Kyle's account and sent him a friend request. Surely, if he was friends with Hannah online, then he would be friends with me too. I also sent a friend request to Hannah, deciding that it would probably be in my best interest to expand my social circle outside of Paige. After a few more minutes of staring at Kyle's two photos and constantly checking to see if he had accepted my friend request yet, I finally fell asleep, but not before letting

Toby and Leo out of Paige's room and cleaning up all the regurgitated treats.

6

Game On

Friday came slower than I had ever imagined, but waking up that morning was exciting, knowing that I would be seeing Kyle. His schedule of only working three days a week gave me limited access to him, but we had a pact, and I couldn't let him down. Without me there to protect him from all the annoying girls, he wouldn't be able to do his job to the best of his ability. I wasn't sure why the Exe Apartments had even hired a security guard for the pool deck since there hadn't been any major incidents since I'd been there, but I was glad that they had. Kyle spent most of his days just checking people's bags and smelling their liquids—a job that I was sure could not be remotely fulfilling—but who was I to judge? I spent all day staring at half-naked models.

I fully wanted to assume the role of Kyle's resident repellent, so as soon as I finished my work for the day, I got ready to head over to the pool. I showered, put on the yellow bikini that I hadn't gotten a chance to wear last weekend, and applied more makeup than usual so that hopefully it would be more noticeable this time. I would have had Paige do it for me if she hadn't already left the apartment for the Thompsons', but then she would've questioned me about why I was getting all dressed up, and I still wasn't ready to tell her about Kyle yet. I grabbed several protein bars and threw them in my bag along with a couple of waters and a book. I wasn't sure how long I was going to be away from my apartment, but I wanted to be prepared.

When I finally made it outside, Kyle was standing by the gate, as expected. His chiseled jawline and upright posture would have given any of the male models I had researched this week a run for their money. The deepness of his voice echoed in my direction, and he greeted me with the most beautiful smile I'd ever seen.

"I have been waiting for you," he proclaimed with the utmost excitement.

"Did you miss me already?" I chirped, excited for what the day had in store for us.

"I thought you might have forgotten about the pact already," he returned teasingly.

"How could I forget? I couldn't miss out on talking to you all day."

Kyle and I continued to exchange pleasantries, and it didn't take long for people to notice that someone had managed to capture his attention. Everyone was so accustomed to seeing him brush off every female's attempt that they were surprised that he seemed to have taken an interest in me. Every time we had to take a pause from our conversation in order for him to tend to his security guard duties, I observed the other girls whispering and staring at me. We weren't dating, but by now everyone knew that if anyone could get Kyle to officially break his rule of not having a relationship with an Exe resident, it was me.

Some women did more than just snicker and talk behind my back. They would give me dirty looks as they passed us by, making it very obvious that they didn't think I was worthy enough to be in the position that I was in. I felt the most uncomfortable when girls would stop to flirt with Kyle right in front of my face. He would smile and play nice, but he didn't engage with them nearly as much as he did with me.

"What are you smiling at?" he innocently asked once he was finally able to catch a break.

"Just happy to be out here with you," I commented.

I wanted Kyle to know that I was interested in him. In my experience, guys didn't make the first move unless they were 100 percent confident that the girl was into them, so I needed to play hard to get while also letting him know that I wanted more than just a friendship.

In the middle of our flirtatious exchange, we were again interrupted, but this time by a hysterical girl who had accidentally sliced her foot on the ledge of the pool. Kyle quickly jumped back into work mode and fetched the first aid kit, then carefully tended to her bloody toe. His eagerness to help and sympathetic nature sent a warmth through my heart. Despite our moment having been interrupted, I couldn't be mad at the situation. He was showing his attentive and caring side, and I couldn't help but imagine what he would be like as a dad. I'd never really wanted kids of my own, but that mindset was slowly shifting with every compassionate move Kyle was making. Besides, if I had them, I could hire Paige as my nanny and live happily ever after with my best friend, Kyle, and our lovely children.

"Sorry about that," Kyle said as he returned from aiding the injured girl. "Duty calls sometimes." He leaned against the pool gate, ready to indulge in more conversation that didn't revolve around someone presumptuously inviting him over to their apartment.

"I hope if I ever need help, you will be there for me too," I told him innocently, even though I was seriously curious about whether or not he would be someone that I could lean on.

"I'll be here whenever you need me," he promised. "I'm only a phone call away."

I paused, realizing there was key information missing. "But I don't even have your number," I pointed out.

"Well, then open your phone," Kyle instructed sincerely.

I pulled it out, unlocked it, and handed it to him. He grabbed it from me and eagerly typed in his number.

"Now you can reach me if you ever need anything," he noted. "Or want anything."

He mischievously smiled, and I was severely intrigued.

"And what exactly would I want from you?" I returned slyly.

Kyle looked me up and down and bit his lip. "Well, I could take the time to explain it to you," he began, "but actions speak louder than words."

I watched him stretch out his hand and gently wrap his fingers around my neck. He applied a minimum amount of pressure, but I could still feel his strength behind the gentle touch. I hadn't been prepared for this moment, and I definitely didn't know how to react, but I remained calm and didn't even flinch. A huge smirk started to emerge across Kyle's mouth as he watched me endure his tightening grip.

"I knew you weren't afraid of a little pain," he proudly whispered as he let go of my neck.

I had spent all of Wednesday night imaging what it would be like when I finally got Kyle's number, but not even in my wildest thoughts could I have fathomed this moment. The sudden hint of violence should've set alarm bells off in my head. I shouldn't have enjoyed his rough handling as much as I did, but it was the first time a guy had touched me since my last relationship. I was craving some sort of physicality. Although light choking wouldn't have been my first choice, I'd still felt a sense of connection to him when his skin met mine. Maybe I was delusional, or maybe I was just desperate for some type of intimate touch. Either way, I wanted to feel him again.

With the sun gone and the pool empty, I enjoyed the last hour of Kyle's shift without any interruptions. It was just him and me under the romantic desert moonlight. If it hadn't been for the serpent tattoo, which assumed its evil persona during the night, it would've been the perfect setting.

"So tell me about your family," Kyle tirelessly asked me. He had been on his feet for almost nine hours in the Vegas heat, so I was surprised he was still able to find the energy to ask me a question about myself.

"I'm an only child," I said. "My dad won the lottery six years ago, and I haven't seen him since." I paused to make sure he was still listening. "He and my mom took the winnings and decided to explore the world. I consider my best friend Paige my only true family."

Kyle was silent. I couldn't tell if he had zoned out or was deeply contemplating my background. After a few quiet moments, he finally spoke up.

"How much did he win?" he asked casually.

"Seventeen million," I responded. "That was six years ago though, so I'm not sure how much of it is left. But they are still traveling, and he still sends me money every month," I reasoned, trying to find a silver lining in having absent parents.

"Interesting," Kyle replied lazily. "Good for him."

I appreciated his effort to try to act interested in my family, but I could tell that he was fighting the urge to fall asleep. To try to keep him awake, I returned the question.

"What about your family?" I asked.

"I have two older brothers," he responded, with a little more energy than before. They must have meant a lot to him, since I saw at least a little flicker of light shine in his eyes at the mention of them.

"My parents tragically died in a fire a few years ago, though," he shared, the light immediately disappearing. "There was an electrical issue with the house, and they weren't able to make it out. Thankfully none of my brothers were home," he added somberly.

"I'm so sorry," I exclaimed with a heavy heart. I knew I had a rocky relationship with my parents, but at least they were still alive.

"It's okay," he replied. "Life is short, so I just try to enjoy it as much as I can." Even in a grieving mood, Kyle was able to find the positive. He had such a sweet heart, and I couldn't believe I got to be in his presence.

We spent the last moments of his shift in a peaceful silence, staring at the stars. I occasionally checked his eyes to make sure he was still awake, which he always met with a slight giggle and reassurance that he was still up.

If my life had been a movie, I would have paused it at this very scene and just soaked it up for as long as I could. Although I could talk to Kyle all day, it was nice to just enjoy a quiet moment together. Just as my eyes were about to close, I was awakened by the sound of the alarm on his phone.

"Shift's over," he announced sluggishly.

Unfortunately, he only worked at the Exe and didn't live there, but at least I had his phone number now. As we both gathered our belongings and made our way toward the exit, he hugged me from behind and whispered in my ear.

"I can't wait to see you tomorrow," he mumbled sweetly.

"Yeah. Maybe one of these days we can actually hang out outside the pool deck," I said.

There was a sudden switch in Kyle's mood. His energy, which had been playful and flirtatious a second ago, turned serious and unamused. He unwrapped his arms from me and turned me around so that I was facing him.

"You are the perfect girl," he began. "I have never met anyone like you, and if I was ready to date someone it would definitely be you, but I'm just not looking for anything serious right now."

His words stung a little bit, and it took me a while to fully digest their meaning. After the amazing day we'd just had, I couldn't tell if he was being serious or was just trying to get a reaction out of me. I knew he didn't date residents, but I hadn't known he wasn't planning on dating at all.

"Well, I'm not looking for anything casual," I returned. Ever since my relationship with Ethan ended, I'd promised myself I wouldn't get involved with another guy unless he was serious about commitment.

"Challenge accepted." Kyle's smile and playful tone returned. He winked at me and headed toward the parking lot.

After tonight, I knew I had at least made a small dent in the wall that Kyle was putting up. In his mind, he wasn't ready to commit to anything serious, but I would show him that I was too great of a girl to pass up until dating me was his only option.

Game on, Kyle Kingsley. Game on.

7
Phone Home

"You got his number?" Paige croaked after taking a swig of her vanilla latte.

"Oh, we definitely have to go to the pool today, then," Hannah suggested after taking a bite of her omelet.

The three of us had decided to enjoy a relaxing Saturday morning brunch at Paige's and my apartment. We were all pretty busy during the week, so it was nice to get together on the weekends. At first, I'd been hesitant to tell them about what had happened, but I'd promised myself that I would only share the specifics of Kyle's and my friendship once there was something noteworthy to tell, and our conversation from the night prior was definitely worth sharing.

I'd told Paige and Hannah almost everything, from the night he'd first caught me staring at him to our secretive pact, and ended with his intentions to keep things casual. I intentionally left out the part where he'd playfully strangled me. It was probably best to keep that little detail to myself. Hannah had a crush on Kyle, so I felt bad divulging some of the story, but she assured me that her feelings toward him were purely superficial and that she was happy for me.

"And you're sure you're okay with him not wanting a serious relationship?" Paige asked hesitantly after I'd finished updating them on my latest gossip.

Paige was the one who'd comforted me throughout my entire breakup with Ethan. I'd been at the lowest point in my life, but she was always there to wipe away my tears and have movie marathons with me until I fell asleep. She'd seen firsthand how badly that relationship destroyed me, and I knew she didn't want to see her best friend hurt again.

I saw the concern in her eyes when I mentioned that Kyle wasn't interested in any sort of commitment. "I think he is just scared of being in a relationship," I muttered through a mouthful of bacon. "Once he gets to know me and realizes that I'm genuinely interested in him, he will probably change his mind."

Hannah looked at Paige to see if my answer satisfied her concerns. Although Hannah hadn't been around when I was grieving my last relationship, I could tell that she was picking up on Paige's apprehension. The two of them would be the first ones to support me in trying to enter the dating world again, but as much as they would have loved to see me with the hot security guard, their number one concern was protecting me. They didn't seem totally convinced that Kyle was worthy of being my next boyfriend.

"I'll give him a chance," Paige finally said, after contemplating the situation. "But if he even thinks about breaking your heart, I'll make sure he never works another day at the Exe again."

"You watch too many crime documentaries," I said with a laugh, reaching for her vanilla latte.

Paige was the most kindhearted person I had ever met, but mess with her family or friends and she turned into the most savage human being ever. She could hold a grudge for the rest of her life and wouldn't stop until she felt justice had been served. I hoped Kyle wouldn't hurt me—not just for my sake, but for his own, because I did not want him to experience the wrath of Paige Jensen.

"If you guys get married, can I plan your bachelorette party?" Hannah asked, offering some comic relief.

"If we get married, you can plan the entire wedding," I proposed jokingly.

The three of us laughed. We enjoyed the rest of our brunch, discussing potential outfit options for the pool party later.

"We can all match!" Paige squealed excitedly. She had three red bikinis in her closet that she was adamant we all wear.

After thoroughly convincing Hannah that redheads can, in fact, wear red, it was decided that we would take the Exe by storm and all three show up dressed in matching swimsuits. We made our way toward Paige's closet, and she rummaged through her drawers to find them. After laying out all three on the bed, Hannah and Paige let me choose the one I wanted first, which was a relief because there was only one that I would actually wear. Paige's taste in swimwear was a lot more unconventional than mine. She preferred styles that were more likely to be found on magazine covers than in real life, so I selected the one that was the most practical.

I ran to my bathroom and quickly changed. Throwing my hair into a high ponytail, I brushed on some light makeup. There was no point in putting too much on, because the sunglasses I had chosen covered most of my face. Ironically, they were one of the most luxurious-looking items I owned, even though I'd bought them from a thrift shop. From far away, they could pass for designer shades.

As I waited in the kitchen for Hannah and Paige to finish getting ready, I realized that I had Kyle's number, but he didn't have mine. I wished I'd possessed the strength to hold off on texting him for longer than the less than twenty-four hours since he'd given it to me, but the temptation was too strong. I reached for my phone, found his contact info, and began crafting a message.

Hi! It's Avery, I wrote. *If you need me to hold up my end of the pact today, just give me a wink. See you at the pool.*

I hit send and quickly put my phone face down, too anxious to see his potential response. As soon as I put it on the table, Hannah and Paige walked out, looking like supermodels. It was obvious Paige had done both of their makeup, because they looked similar in style.

"Whoever said redheads can't pull off red must not have tried on this bikini!" Hannah shouted as she pranced around the kitchen. "I can't believe it took me this long to give the color a chance."

She'd chosen a cutout one-shoulder-style bikini that was comprised of numerous intricate straps and had a huge bow on the back. Paige walked out in an extraordinary one-piece with beautiful gold trim and a few areas made of sheer material.

"You both look stunning," I added, applauding as they entered. "Ten out of ten."

Hannah and Paige walked up and down the kitchen a few more times, strutting as if it were a runway. I grabbed Paige's phone and took several obnoxious pictures of them as if I were the paparazzi. We cracked up over how terrible the photos turned out, but kept them all for the memories.

When we were finally ready to leave, I checked my phone. I had two notifications waiting for me. One was an alert saying Kyle had accepted my friend request, and the other was a text message.

I am definitely going to need you today, Avery.

I smiled to myself as Hannah, Paige, and I left for the pool. The thought of Kyle needing me today made me feel special. I doubted he had this sort of secret deal with any of the other girls that lived here, and it was comforting to know that he valued our pact.

Once we got outside, we were shocked by the amount of people there. The line to enter the pool party wrapped around the entire complex. There was a famous DJ hosting this Saturday's festivities, and it seemed the whole city had decided to show up. The Exe had hired additional security for the event since there were so many residents and guests attending, and I was a little disappointed when we got to the front and someone other than Kyle examined our bags.

Fortunately, Kyle was working the VIP line next to us, so when we walked past him, I flashed a bright smile and gave him a lighthearted wink. He saw me but didn't change his hardened expression and barely even lifted the corners of his mouth. He acted as if he didn't know me and continued to focus his attention on his job.

"What was that all about?" Paige asked when she noticed his lack of reaction.

"He's probably just stressed out." I defended him even though I was a little hurt by his underwhelming response. "I mean, look at all these people," I noted, gesturing toward the crowd.

I really hoped Kyle had just not been in the mood to fraternize after seeing all of the attendees he had to check in rather than purposely disregarding me. There were over a hundred people in line, and the blazing sun wasn't helping either, so I wouldn't have been surprised if he was just exhausted. It was strange to wrap my head around the fact that the guy I had texted a few minutes earlier and the one that had just ignored me were the same person.

"Maybe he didn't see you," Hannah chimed in. She tied her hair up into a ponytail and cleared her throat. "Kyle!" she shouted. "Avery wants to say hi!"

Everyone around us turned to stare. Although there was music blasting through the speakers, it wasn't loud enough to drown out the embarrassing announcement that Hannah had just made. Kyle was glaring over at us while she continued to frantically point at me. I had no other choice than to wave at him, as she showed no signs of letting up until he finally acknowledged me. He eventually removed himself from the VIP line and shuffled toward us. Hannah was evidently proud of her efforts, though I could have done without them.

"Can I help you?" Kyle mumbled when he finally reached us.

"Avery wanted to say hi," Hannah said again, smirking as she gave me an obvious wink and a nudge with her elbow. This had to be one of the most awkward moments of my life, but at least I would get an opportunity to talk to Kyle for a bit.

"I don't know an Avery," he smugly returned, not breaking eye contact with Hannah.

My heart cracked. He was disowning me in front of my friends and didn't even have the courage to look me in the eye while doing it.

"Let's just go and grab a drink," Paige said as she tried to drag us to the bar, but Hannah was too oblivious to catch on to her hint. Her innocence was one of my favorite things about her, but in this instance, it was the very thing that was breaking me inside.

"What do you mean?" Hannah insisted, still looking at Kyle. "She's right here."

She pointed at me, and I immediately wanted to burst into flames. Paige was trying to pull us out of the conversation, but Hannah wasn't letting it go.

Kyle finally turned to me. I tried to catch a glimpse of his sweet soul in his eyes, but they were as empty and deceitful as the ones that his snake tattoo possessed. He looked me up and down a few times before turning back to Hannah.

"Sorry, I don't know your friend," he replied as he walked back to the VIP line.

"What a weirdo," Hannah said, turning to Paige and me. "Okay, let's grab those drinks now!"

She appeared to have dismissed Kyle's unusual behavior, because she quickly moved on and went into party mode, but I knew Paige had taken a mental note. I loved how protective she was over me, but I didn't want her to judge him too quickly. I was hoping it was all just a big misunderstanding, even though the cracks in my heart disagreed.

As we headed over to the bar, the group of girls in front of us did a double take when they saw us. I figured they hadn't expected to see three girls all wearing red bikinis, especially the styles that Hannah and Paige were wearing, but I had definitely seen stranger things at a pool party.

"Are you the girl that's dating Kyle?" one of them finally asked after a few stares.

I knew that it had been obvious that Kyle and I were spending a lot of time together, but I hadn't been expecting anyone to confront me about it.

"We aren't dating," I responded casually. "We're just getting to know each other."

I wasn't going to admit to a stranger that Kyle wasn't interested in anything serious with me and had just rejected me in front of my friends. I liked that we gave off the impression of being in a relationship, and I wasn't totally convinced yet that he really didn't want anything more with me. If he truly wanted to keep things casual, then he wouldn't have spent his entire shift talking to me or given me his number.

"So he's available?" another girl in front of us asked.

I wasn't sure how to answer her question. Of course he was single, but I was really interested in him and didn't want anyone else to get in the way of that.

"He doesn't date residents," Hannah quickly chimed in, the same way she had when she'd first caught me staring at him.

"That's too bad," the girl continued, "but I don't live here."

The women laughed and returned to their original position facing the front of the line. Paige saw the anguish on my face and the stress running through my body. She definitely wasn't going to give Kyle a chance after his behavior today.

"Why don't we just go back to our place and have a mini photo shoot in our cute outfits?" Paige suggested, clearly an attempt to cheer me up.

"Yes, we have honestly never looked better," Hannah agreed, finally picking up on her efforts to change the subject. Taking pictures was probably the last thing I wanted, but leaving the pool sounded like music to my ears.

They both stared at me, waiting for a response. "Fine," I said, "but Toby and Leo have to join in too." I laughed, making light of the situation. I wasn't going to let a guy I barely knew ruin my weekend. I was living in Vegas with my best friend, and I couldn't have been more grateful.

"You stole the words right out of my mouth," Paige told me as we raced toward the exit.

The week flew by, and before I knew it, I was already in the middle of another Wednesday evening spent watching movie marathons while Paige pulled an overnight shift at the Thompsons'. This time I invited Hannah over, but she fell asleep during the fourth movie and then went back to her apartment. She didn't like romantic comedies as much as I did, so I was surprised that she'd even lasted three and a half movies.

It was nice to spend some time with her though, because her presence cheered me up after a terrible workday. My manager was not happy with some of the comments that people were making on our social media pages, so she tasked me with deleting the negative ones. I spent my whole day removing comments regarding how "boring" and "stiff" our models were. There was also backlash on the lack of diversity that our agency presented, but I figured I'd leave those comments up. The company could use some constructive criticism.

After Paige, Hannah, and I had left the party early on Saturday, we didn't go back to the pool that weekend. I figured Kyle would text me to apologize or to ask me to hang out with him during his shift, but he never reached out. I figured the best thing for me to do was to not dwell on it. I'd ask him about his confusing behavior the next time I saw him, but for the time being, it was in my best interest to focus my attention on other things. Besides, I still needed to figure out a way to let Paige's mom know that I wanted to quit my job. I wasn't sure how much longer I could work for Ace Modeling Agency.

After completing my nighttime routine, I hopped into bed with my laptop to review local job listings. Paige's mom couldn't be mad at me if I left my current position because of a better opportunity. I did a quick search for open positions in Las Vegas. As much as I loved working from the comfort of my bedroom, I needed a way to force myself to leave the apartment, so I refrained from clicking on any posts for remote jobs. Most of the ones I saw were located inside hotels, which made me chuckle to myself as I remembered Kyle's comment about me having a crippling fear of casinos.

After an hour of scrolling through endless posts, I closed my laptop for the night. If I was going to apply for jobs, it needed to be after a good night's rest and not at eleven o'clock in the evening. Before I closed my eyes, my phone buzzed. My heart leaped hoping it was Kyle, finally ready to apologize and explain his behavior from the party. To my defeat, the word "Mom" flashed across the screen. I unlocked it, not even the least bit curious about which country they were traveling to next. I navigated toward my mom's recent message and almost threw up when I read her text. I read it ten times before contemplating chucking my phone out the window or throwing it into a fire.

I read her message one more time before deciding that running it over with a car would be my best option.

We are in Vegas! Let's get dinner tomorrow.

8

Dinner Date

When Paige returned to the apartment the following morning, I told her about my mother's text. She didn't approve of my idea to run over my phone with a car, but she did help me try to come up with an excuse not to go.

"You could say that you have pneumonia," Paige offered as she and I paced around the living room, "or that you had a skydiving accident?"

She felt bad that my parents had found out I was in Vegas from her social media. She had posted the picture of her, Hannah, and me in our red bikinis and tagged our location. Evidently, Mom and Dad had taken that as an invitation to reach out to me.

They'd ditched me when I was a teenager to go on an endless vacation, and it wasn't fair that they thought it was okay to just walk back into my life. As much as I wanted to see them again, I wasn't ready for the disappointment of them leaving me for a second time. Who knew how long it would be before I saw them after that?

"Lice!" Paige shouted after I'd shut down all of her previous ideas. "You could say that there was a lice infestation."

I loved that she was trying to help me avoid the dinner, but we were running out of time. My mother followed up her text this morning with the details of the plans, and I still hadn't responded. I figured it was time to face the music and just accept my fate. I pulled out my phone and shakily wrote back to her.

Okay.

After all my parents had put me through, one word was all they deserved. Paige looked at me in dismay. She was stunned that I had given up on our intense brainstorming session, but proud that I was going to reunite with my mom and dad. I tried to beg her to attend the dinner with me, but it was the Thompsons' anniversary tonight, and she had already promised she would watch the kids.

I spent the rest of the afternoon going over every worst-case scenario in my head. If I set the expectations at rock bottom, then the chance of my parents disappointing me would be lower. Paige did my makeup to try to boost my confidence, but it was useless. My parents and I were friends online, so they knew what I had grown to look like over the last six years, but adding a little makeup to cover up a face that they would barely recognize anyway was meaningless.

I finished getting ready and grabbed my stuff to head out the door. Paige went through her usual routine of reminding me to bring my key despite never remembering to take hers. This time I was actually thankful for the reminder, because I'd almost walked out without it. I had lived in the apartment for almost two weeks and never forgotten the key once. Clearly, I wasn't thinking straight.

"I'll be gone when you get back," Paige started, "but tell me everything tomorrow morning!"

"Who is going to lock the door behind you if I'm not home?" I asked as I was leaving.

"I'll remember the key this time," she said with a sincere smile, even though we both knew that wasn't true, as much as I trusted Paige.

However, I wasn't too concerned, because if anyone wanted to break into our apartment, the only treasures they would find would be our coin jar, which was worth roughly fourteen dollars, and a plethora of unconventional bikinis.

I took my time driving over to the restaurant. I was already running late, but I was in no hurry. If I could wait six years for them, then they could wait fifteen minutes for me. After turning a ten-minute drive into a twenty-minute one, I pulled into the parking lot of an old diner, which seemed like an odd choice for a couple worth seventeen million. I'd expected a steakhouse in the middle of the Las Vegas Strip that served their food on plates made of gold, but my parents probably didn't think I was worth the bill.

I slowly exited my car after considering turning around, but I had already made the journey, so I might as well get a free meal out of it. Besides, the proud look on Paige's face when she realized I was going to follow through with the dinner made it worth it.

As I headed toward the diner, my anxiety kicked into overdrive. I had spent the entire afternoon wondering if they would recognize me, but would I even recognize them? I finally calmed my nerves by reminding myself that there would most likely only be one couple in the restaurant dressed in overpriced designer clothes. I made my way inside and approached the hostess table.

"I'm dining with my parents tonight," I announced. "They should already be here."

"Avery?" the hostess asked.

I nodded. My parents must have told her I was coming.

The nice lady walked me over to a table all the way in the back. It was a pretty dimly lit establishment, but when we turned the final corner, I was hoping that the lights would magically turn off completely so that I could escape the disastrous meeting I already knew was waiting for me. There, sitting on the same side of the booth staring at me, were my parents. I hadn't seen them in six years, and they definitely didn't look how I remembered them. My dad's dark hair was receding at the hairline, and he wore glasses now. He wasn't dressed in a luxury suit, but his jacket still looked expensive. My mother had developed crow's feet around both her eyes, and her makeup skills had declined from what I recalled. They didn't look like lottery winners, but maybe they were just hiding their wealth.

"Hi, Mom. Hi, Dad." I greeted them aimlessly, as if this wasn't the first time I had seen them in more than half a decade.

"Avery!" my mom cried out as she tried to inch her way out of the booth to give me a hug.

I shook my head to signal that I was in no mood to embrace her. Instead, I nonchalantly slid into the opposite side of the booth. I'd thought I was going to feel an overwhelming sense of love and affection when I saw them, but the damage had already been done. They'd chosen money over me, and I wasn't able to forgive them for that.

"We're happy to see you," my dad expressed, though he didn't seem too excited. I supposed his monthly checks didn't ease his parenting guilt all the way through.

"Why am I here?" I blatantly stated. "You haven't seen me since I was sixteen, and now all of a sudden you want to have dinner with me?"

This wasn't the time for small talk. I knew my parents had an ulterior motive beyond just catching up with their daughter. At this point, I just wanted to get it over with. I hadn't even looked at the menu and wasn't sure if I was even in the headspace to eat.

"We're so sorry," my mom began. "We have missed you so much, and we wanted to see you."

I shifted my gaze toward my dad. I knew Mom was going to feed me emotional nonsense, but he would give it to me straight. "Why am I actually here?" I repeated again, directing the question at my father.

"We wanted to tell you in person that we won't be traveling anymore," my mother inserted.

Her enthusiastic tone did not work on me. I knew there must be more to the story than that, which was why she felt the need to interject her comments into the conversation before my dad could expose the truth.

I ignored my mother's failed attempt to try and soften the blow. We waited in silence until Dad was ready to share what had happened.

"I lost all of our money," he admitted, bowing his head in shame.

I looked toward my mother, who nodded in confirmation. "The dealer cheated," she uttered in his defense.

I should have known that my dad wasn't cured of his gambling addiction just because he'd won the lottery. A man who would trade his relationship with his only daughter for some money should not have taken a trip to Las Vegas. There was temptation everywhere. If only he'd had a crippling fear of casinos.

"So now what?" I asked, wondering what his gambling losses had to do with me. It was obvious that I wouldn't be receiving the monthly checks anymore, but other than that, I wasn't sure how this affected my life.

"We were wondering if we could stay with you until we can get back on our feet," my mom said. "It would only be for a little while."

The audacity. My parents believed that I was naive enough to let them live with me. They'd abandoned me at sixteen and were now crawling back into my life, begging for a place to stay. They hadn't wished me a happy birthday, called me on Christmas, or told me they loved me in years, and now they wanted my help. They could take the money they had left to buy a bus ticket to La-La-Land, because there was no chance that I was going to let them live with me.

Without giving them an answer, I nonchalantly gathered my belongings and slid to the end of the booth. I was clearly not going to accept their proposal, so there was nothing left to discuss. As I was about to stand up, the waitress came over to our table.

"Can I get you guys anything to drink?" she interrupted, unaware that a family fallout was occurring at the table.

My mother looked at me as I stood up to leave. "Could we have some money for dinner?" she asked in a pitiful tone. "It's the least you could do with all the money your father sent you."

I reached into my pocket, dug out my car keys, and threw my purse over my shoulder. In a calm and unwavering tone, I turned to my parents and muttered, "Over my dead body," then stormed out of the restaurant.

When I got into my car, I pulled out my phone to call Paige. My vision was becoming blurred from the tears, but as I unlocked my phone, I could make out the word "Kyle" staring back at me from my screen.

Meet me at the pool tomorrow.

Great, another person that wants to come back into my life.

9
Trouble in Paradise

I rolled out of bed Friday morning with a headache and puffy eyes. If I'd been brave enough to look into the mirror, I probably wouldn't have recognized myself. Once Paige returned home from the Thompsons', I cried my eyes out in her lap. We both knew how selfish my parents were, but neither of us had been expecting them to ask to move in with me after all they had done. It was obvious that any ounce of relationship I had with them was now gone. I didn't care that they were no longer traveling the world, or that my father wouldn't be sending me any more money.

When I first woke up, I felt slightly guilty for having denied my parents a place to stay, but immediately snapped out of it when I remembered how quick they'd been to leave me behind. I showered and tried to make myself look as presentable as possible, even though I hadn't even gotten around to brushing my hair. I tied it into a knot on top of my head and threw on a baggy outfit. I took the day off work, which my manager wasn't too happy about due to the late notice, but her opinion was the least of my concerns. It was Friday, which meant Kyle was working today, but I had no interest in trying to dazzle him with a cute bikini. This disheveled look would have to do.

I followed the scent of sweet-and-savory deliciousness coming from the kitchen and found Paige and Hannah making my favorite breakfast; cinnamon rolls and bacon. I couldn't remember the last time Paige had consumed anything other than coffee for her morning meal, but she always put aside her own feelings in order to make sure I was happy.

It was also nice to see Hannah's cheery face, although I was pretty confident that Paige hadn't explained the full story. I didn't think anyone could wrap their head around how parents could forsake their only child for six years only to return to beg for a place to stay.

"Good morning!" Paige shouted as she ran up to give me a hug. "Care for some breakfast?" She flashed a piece of bacon under my nose.

"I'll take three," I answered, grabbing the meat from her hand. "And two cinnamon rolls, please," I requested as she made me a plate.

I took my place at the kitchen table and sat next to Hannah.

"Wow, you look terrible," she observed when she noticed my unkempt appearance.

Hannah quickly covered her mouth in embarrassment. Clearly, she hadn't meant to let that comment slip, but I actually thought it was kinda funny hearing it from her. She was the nicest person in the world, and it always caught me off guard when anything other than sweet compliments left her tongue.

"It's okay," I reassured her, "I know I look like I haven't slept in days."

"More like months," Hannah corrected.

We both laughed, and for a second, I almost forgot about all of the drama in my life.

"Eat up!" Paige exclaimed as she placed the most delicious-smelling breakfast in front of me.

I dove into my plate and inhaled my food. I hadn't eaten since lunch yesterday, and my stomach was in need of some nutrition. My mind was so preoccupied with eating that I almost didn't hear Hannah over my obnoxious chewing.

"Paige and I are painting today," she revealed as she pointed to the art supplies sitting on the couch. "Want to join us?"

I stared at the large plastic bag filled with canvases, paints, paintbrushes, easels, and stencils. Toby and Leo were also curious about it, but I think they were more interested in the bag than the actual contents.

"Maybe later," I murmured quietly. "I'm actually meeting Kyle at the pool soon."

Paige gave me an unimpressed look. She didn't need to utter a word—I could read the disappointment all over her face.

"Why are you hanging out with Kyle?" Paige asked. "I thought you were done with him."

"I was, but he texted me last night and asked me to meet him by the pool today," I stuttered. I stared at the empty plate in front of me. I didn't have the courage to look Paige in the eye.

"Do you want to bring him some bacon?" Hannah asked, not understanding the severity of the situation. She didn't hold grudges the way Paige did, so I wasn't surprised she was oblivious to the fact that Kyle was on my best friend's hit list.

"Don't worry, it will all be fine," I reassured Paige as I stood up from the table. "He most likely just wants to apologize for his behavior at the pool party." I grabbed one more piece of bacon and swiftly headed for the door before she could lecture me any further.

"Save me a canvas," I added as I exited the apartment. "I probably won't be gone long."

The lonely walk through the hallways allowed me the uninterrupted time I needed to let my thoughts flood my brain. I had never fully processed the idea that I didn't have a relationship with my parents anymore, and so far, the friendship that I had with Kyle was doing more harm than good. I couldn't wait until the conversation with him was over, because I could really use some art therapy.

I pushed through the door to enter the pool deck and saw him waiting by the gate. He was easy to find since he was at his usual spot and no other residents were outside yet. I walked over to him in my baggy sweatpants with my puffy eyes and leaned against the gate, not facing him.

"Nice day today," Kyle began, which broke the silence between us.

"Sure is," I replied nonchalantly.

"I haven't seen you in a while." He smiled. "What happened to our pact?"

He maintained his casual attitude and relaxed demeanor. I was starting to believe he didn't even realize how he'd acted or know that I was upset with him, which made me even more angry. I kept my eyes focused on the still water and empty pool chairs as I confronted him.

"You know you basically rejected me in front of my friends at the party last week," I started. "You acted like you didn't even know who I was."

Kyle was quiet as he seemed to be trying to remember the previous weekend. An event that I thought was pretty unforgettable took him a minute to even recall. After several moments, he finally realized what I was talking about and began to defend himself.

"I'm sorry," he said. "My boss yelled at me for spending too much time with you, and I didn't want to get in trouble again."

My anger eased slightly, but I wasn't ready to let him off the hook yet. I was still incredibly embarrassed and hurt over the situation.

"You could have at least told me or texted me after," I pointed out.

I still wasn't able to look him in the eye, but I could tell his body language had softened and that he hadn't realized how much his actions had affected me.

"I feel terrible," Kyle told me. "If I'd known how bad it would make you feel, I would have never done it. I'm so sorry. I wish I could take it all back."

I could hear the sincerity in his voice, and it pained me to know that we were both upset over a misunderstanding.

"It's fine," I said solemnly. "I forgive you."

"How can I make it up to you?" he asked eagerly.

We stood in silence for a while as I contemplated this. I was still upset that he hadn't explained the situation earlier, but I knew I had been too quick to judge him over one minor incident.

"Well, I could take the time to explain it to you," I playfully murmured as I moved closer to him, "but actions speak louder than words."

With that, Kyle wasted no time, and in one swift movement, he grabbed me and lifted me toward his mouth. My heart was thumping out of my chest as he inched his face closer to mine. He pursed his lips slightly and intensified his grip around me. I was inches away from crashing my mouth into his, but right as our lips were about to touch, he looked down at me and took in my soul through his eyes. He analyzed my face before eventually deciding to let me go and replace the original distance between us.

"Was I hurting you?" he asked, studying my expression. "You look like you are about to cry."

Ugh, I should have put more effort into getting ready this morning. My puffy eyes and flushed face were ruining my moment with Kyle.

"I'm fine," I said. "My parents were just in town."

Kyle's eyes filled with concern, and he no longer seemed interested in my lips. My mom and dad were out of the picture, but they were still finding a way to steal my happiness. I decided to briefly share what happened at dinner so that Kyle and I could try to return back to the romantic moment that we'd almost shared.

"It was emotional seeing them for the first time since high school," I explained.

Kyle's face didn't change. He was still showing a great deal of concern, so in an effort to lighten the mood, I altered the details of the story slightly.

"They were just stopping by to let me know that they were going to be gone again for a while, but before they left, they gave me an envelope with two tickets to Paris in it," I lied.

This still didn't shake Kyle from his sadness. I realized I would have to adjust the story even further to ease his worries.

"And twenty-five thousand in cash," I added.

This was enough to snap him out of his depressed state.

"Twenty-five thousand dollars?" he repeated. "I would cry too."

We both laughed and proceeded to list all the things we would do with the money. I'd successfully brought the life back into Kyle, but not the romance. Our first kiss would have to wait a little longer.

We spent a few more hours laughing and fantasizing about our newfound rich lifestyle, until the pool started to get busy. Kyle was distracted by the influx of residents showing up, so I decided it was time to head back down to my apartment and see if Paige and Hannah were still painting. I waited for Kyle to inspect the last girl's bag before letting him know that I was leaving.

"Wow, you have such beautiful eyes," the girl teased as Kyle rummaged through her stuff. "I'm so jealous of you."

I wasn't surprised by her observation, since Kyle's eyes were absolutely gorgeous, but she wasn't the first and she wouldn't be the last person to comment on them. I started walking toward him in order to stop the nonsense. We had a deal, and I had to rescue him before he was in too deep.

Kyle caught me out of the corner of his eye and gently shook his head at me. I was surprised by his dismissal, but I assumed he wanted to handle this one on his own. When the girl finally left, he ran up to me, beaming with happiness.

"Guess what?" He smirked as he waved his phone in front of my face. "I just got her number."

I was stunned. He'd made it very clear that he wasn't looking for anything serious, especially with a resident, so I was confused as to why he had gotten her number. Not to mention, he'd almost kissed me a few minutes ago.

"What about our pact?" I nervously stammered. "I tried to save you."

"Don't worry, Avery. You didn't have to save me from her," he assured me as he peered over the pool gate to get another good look at the girl. "She's cute, right?"

"So cute," I whispered, my heart aching.

"You think she would go out with me?" Kyle genuinely asked.

The entire chain of events was unsettling, and I could feel an ache in the back of my throat threatening to come out in the form of tears. We had just finished clearing the air and almost kissed, and now he was getting another girl's number. I thought I had made progress with him, but he was making it very clear that my efforts were meaningless.

"So you're willing to go on a date with her but not me?" I blurted out, enraged and hurt. I hadn't been planning on letting my emotions get the best of me, but my heart couldn't take it anymore. I couldn't let Kyle break me more than he already had.

"I value what we have so much that I don't want to ruin it by dating," he answered. "I know you are looking for a serious relationship, and that is just something I can't give you right now. I thought we had an understanding?"

I stared at my feet, not wanting to show him my true emotions, but each word he spoke pierced through my heart. We had both made our intentions clear from the beginning, but I'd been hoping I could change his. I'd been hoping things would be different.

"You're right," I acknowledged as I wiped away an escaping tear. "You were honest from the start, and I should respect your boundaries."

I turned away from him and headed toward the exit, intending to avoid any further conversation, but Kyle grabbed my hand and pulled me close to him.

"I'm too broken," he whispered. "All I would do is hurt you."

I appreciated his honesty, but I wished he would have let me come to that conclusion on my own. We both carried baggage from our past, but I was willing to accept all of his flaws.

"I like you for exactly who you are," I assured. "Your imperfections don't scare me. You're not too damaged. We are perfectly broken in our own ways, and I'm willing to put your pieces back together if you're willing to do the same for me."

Kyle stared at me, speechless.

"I want you and everything that comes with it," I confessed. I looked up at him so that he could see the sincerity in my expression and the truth in my voice.

"Everything?" he asked.

"Everything," I confirmed.

Kyle's demeanor slowly softened, and I could have sworn that I witnessed a tiny wall that was protecting his heart crumble right before my eyes.

"You have no idea what you're in for, Avery," he hesitantly informed me. "Don't say I didn't warn you."

"Warn me about what?" I asked, but I don't think Kyle heard me, as my words were swallowed by his mouth, which came crashing down onto mine in a wave of passionate desire. His tongue was sloppy, and his hands were reaching for areas that were off-limits. I couldn't find a rhythm because he was inconsistent in his movements. Nothing about the kiss was soft or sensual. His teeth were clanking against mine, and he was aggressive in his maneuvers. If it had been anyone else, I probably would have pulled away by now, but I wanted nothing more than to finally earn a chance to be more than friends with Kyle. I figured this was the first step in the right direction; therefore, despite the chaotic make-out session, it was the best first kiss ever.

10
Cooking up a Storm

As much as I loved a delicious sweet-and-savory breakfast to start the morning, it was way harder to make than to eat. I had already burnt a batch of cinnamon rolls and a package of bacon before ten, and the fire alarms were exhausted from blaring at all my failed attempts. Paige was sitting at the kitchen table, quietly reading a fashion magazine and inhaling the oven fumes. She'd passed on her vanilla latte this morning when she noticed that the milk was a week past its due date. Instead, she'd decided to take the opportunity to watch me fail miserably in the kitchen as she refused to help me cook breakfast for Kyle. Her grudge against him held firmly, and one kiss wasn't enough to change her mind.

My relationship with Kyle had clearly been solidified last night. The walls he had up to protect his heart were slowly being let down, and he was finally opening up to the idea of being part of a relationship that was more serious than a casual friendship. I didn't think we were officially together yet, but the kiss said a lot more than anything he could have ever verbalized. He didn't have to tell me how he felt; he'd shown me with his actions. We were finally headed in the right direction.

"I think you should just bring him the burnt bacon crisps stuck to the bottom of the pan," Paige suggested. "He could wash it down with my expired milk."

I rolled my eyes as I opened the fridge, searching for ingredients to make a sandwich. Surely, even someone like me couldn't mess that up.

After the kiss with Kyle, I wanted to do something nice to show him that I truly meant what I said. No matter what, I was going to stick by his side through all of his imperfections. I figured bringing him breakfast, which was now turning into lunch, would be a kind gesture to brighten his day before a long shift.

"Do you think he's more of a ham or turkey guy?" I asked Paige as I held the two deli meats in the air.

"I'd guess ham," Paige answered. "He acts like a pig, so he probably likes to eat it too."

I continued to ignore her comments and opted for the turkey. Kyle was going to have to perform some sort of a grand gesture in order to get back on Paige's good side.

"You know he's not that bad," I retorted.

"Oh, right," Paige argued, "he just likes to publicly ignore you and then get another girl's number right in front of your face."

I was over her rude remarks. She didn't have to like Kyle, but her harsh comments were unnecessary.

"He apologized," I corrected. "It was all just a misunderstanding."

"Well, it won't be a misunderstanding when I—"

"Enough!" I yelled. "You're just mad that a guy picked me over you for once!"

I knew I had gone too far, but the words came out faster than I could take them back. It wasn't fair for me to take my insecurities out on Paige. She'd been nothing but a supportive friend and never made dating a competition between us. I cautiously watched her as she silently stood from the kitchen table and walked back to her room. I frantically apologized as she was leaving, but the last thing she wanted was to hear from me. I had crossed the line this time.

"Next time he hurts you," Paige said as she disappeared into her room, "don't come crying to me."

She slammed the door behind her, which sent a rattling throughout the kitchen. The knife I was using for Kyle's sandwich clanked as it hit the ground from the sudden jolt. It left a trail of mayonnaise in its path. I reached for the paper towels to clean up the mess, but the bigger mess between Paige and me wasn't going to be fixed that easily.

I hated when Paige and I fought. She was my best friend, and I couldn't stand her being mad at me. I was one of the few people in the world that she never held a grudge against. I immediately wanted to run into her room and apologize, but I needed to get the sandwich up to Kyle before his shift started and the craziness of the party began. I figured by the time I returned, Paige would have cooled down and we could go back to laughing and being friends again. We never stayed angry at each other for long. The last time she and I fought had been sophomore year of high school, when her brother Graham and I decided to pull a prank on her and fill her shampoo bottle with ketchup. Despite many failed attempts to get the smell out of her hair, she still didn't stay mad at us for long.

After adding the last slice of bread on top, I grabbed my pathetic excuse for a sandwich and left the apartment. The ratio of ingredients was slightly skewed, since we'd only had one slice of turkey left and the abundance of condiments were the direct result of my heavy-handedness. When I opened the door to the pool deck, I noticed I had poked a hole through the bread from gripping it too hard. Mayonnaise was gushing out the sides, and I debated whether I should even give him the sandwich at that point, but I thought he would at the very least find it funny.

I scanned the deck for Kyle and eventually spotted him by the pool. His hair was neatly tucked under his baseball cap, and the way his biceps screamed when he turned it backwards was enough to make my heart throb. It wasn't until I finally pulled myself together that I realized he was standing over the water, talking to the girl whose number he had gotten yesterday. She was cheerfully swishing around and laughing at everything he was saying. I tried not to jump to conclusions, but I could feel a wave of disappointment flow through me. I took my anger out on the sandwich as it crumbled beneath my tightening grip. Still using the bread as a stress ball, I slowly inched my way toward them. By the time I made it over, it was nothing but a pile of mush.

"Everything okay?" Kyle asked, eyeing the deconstructed sandwich in my hand.

"Everything is great," I managed to respond through my teeth.

I didn't want to let on how anxious I was feeling, but seeing Kyle with another girl made my stomach churn. Maybe I had misread the significance of our kiss. I was really trying to give him the benefit of the doubt, but it was exhausting going through this emotional roller coaster with him. The highs and lows were overwhelming, and I wanted to get off the ride.

"I brought you some food," I sorrowfully proclaimed as I held up the crumbled disaster.

"Thank you." Kyle chuckled as he observed my filthy hands. "Hold on, let me grab you a napkin."

As much as I was grateful for his kindness, I felt my face flush in defeat. This had not gone the way I'd envisioned it. He was supposed to warmly accept a delectable sandwich crafted from the heart. It was intended to signify my commitment to him, and instead it just showed that I couldn't cook. The thoughtful gesture had turned into a messy disaster, and I was now left alone with a girl who had an obvious interest in Kyle. I stared at her in the thick of an awkward silence before she eventually broke it.

"I'm Jessica," she said, wading through the water.

"Avery," I returned.

Jessica was too far away to shake hands with unless I bent down, so I just smiled at her, still holding a fistful of crushed bread. Her platinum blonde hair floated in the water, which prompted me to question Kyle's type. He claimed we were both cute, but Jessica and I looked nothing alike. She was peppered with tiny tattoos and tasteful piercings that complemented her slender body. Her beauty caused me to question my own attractiveness and diminished my confidence in Kyle's level of interest in me.

"Oh, I know who you are," Jessica confirmed. "Kyle talks a lot about you."

I was surprised, but I blushed at the idea of him bringing me up in conversation. I knew our feelings had grown with our kiss last night, but I hadn't expected him to mention me to her.

"Do you guys live together?" she innocently inquired.

I found it a little presumptuous of her, but I figured these were normal questions people asked, and I was excited for the opportunity to talk about Kyle and me.

"I live here," I answered, "but Kyle only works here."

I realized that I didn't actually know where Kyle lived. I would have to ask him about that later if I was going to keep getting bombarded with these types of questions.

"He probably did that on purpose so he could watch over you." Jessica gleamed.

"Well, we are very protective of each other," I confirmed.

This girl seemed super sweet and genuinely interested in our relationship. Talking to her made me thankful that I hadn't turned the sandwich into ammo and thrown it at Kyle's head when I first walked out onto the pool deck. He was obviously just excited about our new relationship and couldn't wait to share it with someone. I didn't blame him. Once Paige and I were on speaking terms again and she finally accepted that Kyle and I were together, I couldn't wait to rant and rave about him. Hannah would get an earful too the next time I saw her.

"I was going to pursue Kyle, but I saw you two were hanging out a lot," Jessica admitted. She continued to aimlessly swish around in the water. I didn't know how to respond, but she didn't seem too upset over it. "I was surprised when he told me that you were just his sister."

"Excuse me?" I cried out. My brain was trying to make sense of what she'd just said.

"I'm sorry," Jessica said. "I'm sure it's weird to hear a girl crushing over your brother."

I was caught completely off guard. It was impossible that Kyle could have told her we were siblings. We'd had our first kiss just last night, so there was no chance he had already gone back on his actions.

"He told you I was his sister?" I blurted out in shock.

"Oh my, is it a secret?" Jessica frantically stumbled over her words. "Don't worry, I won't tell anyone." Her face had a confidential expression, as if she possessed inside information. "Should I also not tell anyone that your dad won the lottery and that you both are young millionaires?" she whispered. "Seventeen million is crazy."

Kyle returned with the napkins and dragged over a trash can so that I could throw the mushy sandwich away. The conversation with Jessica had made me forget about the repulsive food remnants still in my hand. Before discarding the sandwich, I contemplated following through with my initial plan of aiming it at Kyle's head. He would have deserved every second of the mayonnaise and turkey revenge. I quickly shifted my attention and forcefully snatched the napkins out of his hand.

"Are you both getting along?" Kyle awkwardly joked.

"Yes, your sister is amazing," Jessica affirmed as she continued to float around the pool.

Kyle's eyes widened, and his stance shifted. He scratched the back of his neck and tried to force a smile.

If looks could kill, right then Kyle would have been dead, because my eyes were burning holes through his skin. I tried to control my emotions, but I could feel the frustration starting to emerge. I turned to leave before I plotted any more retaliations.

Kyle grabbed my arm and pulled me back toward him. He had an apologetic look on his face, and his eyes were enchanting me to forgive him.

"It's not what it looks like," he stammered, trying to reassure me.

I wanted to believe him, but I couldn't find the energy to endure another emotional ride. I removed my arm from his grip and created space between us.

"Thanks for the napkins," I managed to croak, before darting for the exit.

As soon as I was out of view, I sprinted down the hall. I was met with insults and curses as I almost knocked over several of the residents' dogs. My only focus was on getting back to my apartment, and I had forgotten that Paige and I were not on speaking terms. When I unlocked our door, I noticed her door was open, so I didn't bother knocking. I gingerly wandered in and quietly sat at the foot of her bed. I knew there was a look of pain and anguish in my eyes. Paige studied my face, but didn't say a word. Her forgiving expression showed that our fight from earlier was over, and she was ready to be my friend again. I scooted toward her and collapsed into her lap.

"He hurt me again," I cried.

11
Party Foul

"That's it—I quit," Hannah grumbled as she twisted the cap back on the expired milk. "This is officially the worst game ever invented."

After an emotionally exhausting day, Paige and I had invited Hannah over for a sleepover and romantic-movie marathon with a twist; every time the characters kissed, we had to take a sniff of Paige's expired milk. I wasn't sure why we hadn't disposed of it yet, but it made for an interesting party game. Unfortunately, we hadn't fully thought it through, and we all ended up with upset stomachs and raging headaches halfway through the first movie.

"How about we just do face masks instead?" Paige suggested as she queasily stood up from the couch and headed toward the bathroom.

"Why couldn't we have just started with that?" Hannah complained, hunching over and grabbing her midsection. She obviously had the weakest stomach of the three of us.

The rotten milk was disgusting, but spending so much time with Paige over the years had forced me to also spend a lot of time with her brother Graham. Since I'd grown up an only child, I didn't know what it was like to live with a guy other than my father. Graham had exposed me to the lifestyle of a teenage boy, and it was definitely worse than a few sniffs of old dairy.

A few moments later, Paige returned with the face masks and a tray of cucumbers. The sight of food repulsed Hannah, but I, on the other hand, was overjoyed. I grabbed a few off the plate and popped them into my mouth.

"They are supposed to be for your eyes," Paige pointed out with a giggle as she took a bite of one herself.

We spent the next few minutes applying our face masks and allowing our eye lids to be shielded by cucumbers. Paige played her relaxing mediation music over the speakers, filling the apartment with peaceful vibes. Even Toby and Leo were basking in the serenity. I was in such a relaxed state that I was hesitant to check my phone when I felt it buzzing in my pocket, but after the second vibration, curiosity got the best of me. I removed one of the cucumbers and pulled it out. There was a text from Kyle.

Sorry for earlier.
Going out tonight and I want you to come.

I was so mentally exhausted from all the ups and downs that his apology meant little to me. I wasn't sure how much longer I could be around his inconsistent behavior. The thought of how he would potentially hurt me next haunted me; however, his spontaneous invitation to hang out slightly piqued my interest. We had never been around each other outside of the pool area, and I would have been lying if I said I wasn't curious about what a night out in Vegas would look like with him. Maybe the Exe was a toxic environment for him and he was a completely different person outside of the premises.

I wasn't sure how Paige would react if I told her that I was going out with Kyle tonight after I had just soaked her sheets in tears, but I weighed the pros and cons and figured this was a once-in-a-lifetime opportunity. Kyle usually had good reasons for his behavior, and I didn't want to shut him down now that he'd finally found someone to open up to. Everyone deserved a second chance, and there was a possibility that this time things would be different.

I accepted his invitation, and he immediately responded with his address. It was exciting knowing that I was finally going to get to see where he lived. Kyle said I should meet him at his apartment an hour after his shift was over, which only gave me a short amount of time to remove the face mask, get dressed, and craft an explanation that Paige would understand. Surprisingly, it didn't take long for me to formulate a plan. I wasn't usually the best liar, but I was so eager to see Kyle that my brain was working in overdrive.

I scanned the room to make sure Paige and Hannah were still distracted by the face masks. Toby and Leo were the only ones aware of my actions, but thankfully my secrets were safe with them. I removed the cap from the expired milk and took a huge sniff before screwing the lid back on. The scent of rotten dairy filled my nostrils, and I was afraid that my brave attempt to get into character was going to backfire.

"Mm, I don't feel so good," I murmured as I held my stomach.

My mediocre acting skills were coming into play as I gingerly stood up from the couch and wobbled in the direction of my room. Paige and Hannah removed their cucumbers and watched me give my award-winning performance.

"Are you okay?" Hannah called after me.

I shook my head and let out a few more groans to further sell my act.

"How can I help?" Paige asked. "Can we get you anything?"

I continued to maintain a weakened walk and nauseated look on my face as I approached my door.

"I'm okay," I moaned, still holding my stomach. "The milk just got the best of me tonight."

"I knew it was a horrible game," Hannah reiterated. She was grabbing her own stomach as the memory of the horrible stench of the milk returned, becoming sick all over again.

"Well, let us know if you need anything, Avery," Paige said with a concerned look on her face.

"I will, thank you." I finished off my act with a few dry heaves. "I will see you both in the morning."

I closed the door behind me with a sigh of relief. Before racing to my closet to find something to wear, I patted myself on the back and completed a few bows in honor of my dramatization. I felt bad for lying to my friends, but who knew when Kyle would ask to see me outside of work again? It was a rare opportunity. I wasn't ignoring the fact that earlier in the day he'd told another girl I was his sister, but he had admitted to the brokenness inside him. He just needed a little guidance in the realm of relationships.

I put on my cutest pair of mom jeans paired with a black crop top and mini black heels. My outfit resembled one that Paige wore often, so I was confident that it was the appropriate attire. I added some curls to my hair and finished off the look with a light dusting of makeup and a purse that matched my shoes. With a final turn in the mirror, I swiftly locked my bedroom door and raced out to the back patio. Paige and I each had a door in our rooms that lead to the outside. We'd chosen these units on purpose so that Toby and Leo could easily explore. They were not intended for me to sneak out to meet up with a boy, but it worked out in my favor.

Once outside, I took a route to the parking lot that didn't pass by our apartment windows and slithered my way into my car to drive off to my destination. Kyle lived roughly twenty minutes away, but my nerves made it feel like an hour. I was so stressed about how the night would turn out that I chose to play some of Paige's meditation music.

When I arrived at Kyle's apartment complex, it was a maze, and it took me a while to find the unit that belonged to him. They all looked similar in the dark, and the lack of personal decoration made it even more confusing. After getting lost a couple of times, I eventually found the right one. The decaying door was unlocked and slightly cracked to allow easy access for Kyle's guests, but I still opted to knock. It didn't matter, though, because I couldn't even hear my own fist banging against the cold wood over the loud music blaring from inside. After standing there for a while, I realized nobody was going to let me in, so I made the conscious decision to enter on my own. I hesitantly pushed open the door and walked into the apartment, revealing three guys and two girls hanging out in the living room.

"Avery!" Kyle shouted as he made his way over to me. "I'm glad you're here!" He greeted with me a hug as if he hadn't just hurt my feelings earlier in the afternoon. "Everyone, this is Avery!" he announced, with his arm around me.

I was met with a bunch of greetings and smiles, which I returned with a bashful wave.

Kyle was one of the most beautiful humans I had ever seen, but his living situation was quite the opposite. The apartment was littered with empty bottles and crushed pizza boxes. There was paint chipping off the walls, and the carpet, which looked as if it had once been white, was now a shade of ugly gray. I could tell the place wasn't as extravagant as the one I shared with Paige, but the lack of furniture and abundance of garbage made it look ten times worse. There was a horrible stench, and the space looked like it hadn't been cleaned in ages. I chose to hang out around the kitchen even though everyone else was gathered on the living room couch. I didn't trust the number of bacteria living inside that sofa, and the kitchen was relatively clean compared to the rest of the apartment.

Kyle was lazily clinging to me as he explained who everyone was. I could tell he was drunk, but I liked how possessive he was being.

"The two guys over there are my older brothers, Eli and Mike." Kyle pointed. "They live in Sacramento, but are in town for the weekend."

I observed the two men wrestling on the couch. All three brothers resembled each other with their tall, muscular frames, golden eyes, and blonde hair.

"And the two girls," Kyle drunkenly continued, "are their girlfriends, Ashley and Layla."

I let out a sigh of relief. I'd had enough female competition for the day, and I was excited to enjoy this night out without any more.

"So we are going out with two couples," I noted as Kyle took another sip from his drink.

"Almost three," he said with a wink as he planted a kiss on my forehead.

"I'm just your sister, remember?" I pointed out sarcastically.

Kyle scratched the back of his neck, which I was starting to gather was a nervous tic of his. I could tell he wanted to avoid the topic, but I wasn't going to be able to enjoy the night without an explanation.

"I was just trying to test your loyalty," he explained. "You said that you would accept me with all of my flaws, and I wanted to see if that was actually true."

I didn't appreciate his attempt to hold me to my word, but I could tell it was the result of having been hurt in the past. It wasn't my place to judge anyone for how they handled their grief. I surely hadn't been in a good frame of mind after my relationship with Ethan.

"I meant what I said," I insisted, "but please don't ever do that to me again."

"I got you, Avery, don't worry," Kyle reassured me as he offered me a sip of his beverage.

"I don't drink, remember?"

"Who lives in Vegas and doesn't drink?" he teased, just like the first time he'd said it.

He was still loosely clinging to me and decided to cover my face with drunken kisses, plastering his saliva all over my lips and neck. It was even sloppier than the first time he'd kissed me, which I'd thought was impossible. If his ID hadn't fallen out of his pocket, I wasn't sure if he ever would have stopped.

"Not again!" Kyle groaned as he bent down to pick the card off the ground.

His drunken state was causing him to overreact, but I could tell trying to safely secure his belongings in his pocket was causing him a lot of stress.

"I can put it in my purse if you want," I offered as he looked for an alternate place to safeguard it. His shallow pockets were clearly not forgiving enough to contain the size of his ID.

"I knew I liked you for a reason." Kyle sluggishly handed it over.

He continued to shower me with compliments and affection until his brother Eli announced that it was time to go to the bars. Eli was clearly the oldest. His face showed more signs of aging than either of his siblings', and he took charge with the bossiness of an eldest child. He had no problem being the authority figure as he rounded up everyone in the apartment. Ashley was evidently his girlfriend, since I watched him grab her waist to guide her out the door. Her blonde hair and tall stature resembled that of the Kingsley brothers', but her ocean eyes set her apart.

Mike, the middle child, was more energetic and talkative than his siblings. He loved the spotlight, and his loud, boisterous voice signaled a yearning for attention. I could tell that his girlfriend, Layla, spent a lot of their relationship simply trying to tame him. He was quite the handful. Layla was not only patient, but she was also beautiful. Her long curly brown hair complemented her hazel eyes. She was wearing a similar outfit to mine, and her bubbly personality reminded me of Paige's. I knew I would get along with her.

Thankfully, the bars were within walking distance, so we didn't have to pile into my tiny car, seeing as I was the only one fit to drive. I don't think I could have survived a drive through the heart of Las Vegas with five overly intoxicated passengers. During the entire stroll there, Kyle was holding my hand and giving me his full attention. He was a different person outside of work hours, and I was hoping that I would get to see more of this side of him in the future.

When we finally arrived, Mike, Eli, Ashley, and Layla darted for the dance floor, but Kyle wanted to hang back and spend some more alone time with me. He took me to a dark section of the bar and continued to shower me with passionate kisses and lustful touches. I wasn't a huge fan of public displays of affection, so I was limiting his actions, but I could tell he would have done a lot more if I'd let him. The other couples were dancing and singing to the live music, but Kyle was trying to have another slobbery make-out session.

I truly enjoyed the seemingly endless attention, but I would have rather been dancing with his brothers and their girlfriends. My private moment with Kyle was becoming increasingly uncomfortable, since he obviously wasn't satisfied with the amount of physical attention he was getting in return. I was afraid to tell him to slow down in case it hurt his feelings or made him put his walls back up, but he was groping me a little too much. When his hands started making their way under my bra, I knew it was time to stop him.

"What's wrong?" Kyle asked, finally taking a break from trying to kiss me. He could tell I was resisting him, but it only made him strengthen his affectionate pursuit.

"Nothing," I said in an attempt to hide my discomfort. "Do you want to dance?"

He turned to locate his brothers on the dance floor. "No, I'm okay, but you go ahead." Kyle pouted. "I'm going to grab another drink."

He left me alone in the dark corner and headed for the bar. I had no other choice but to aimlessly follow him or rejoin the others. I chose the latter and maneuvered my way through the crowd to dance alongside Layla, Ashley, and the other two Kingsley brothers. We had only been enjoying the music for a few short moments when Kyle showed up. He wasn't as touchy-feely as he had been earlier, which I was thankful for, until I realized that it was because he'd decided to redirect his affection toward someone who was able to reciprocate. The girl next to him was more than willing to accept his persistent advances, and she wasted no time in grabbing his face. Before I could even react, they were aggressively making out right next to me. She even bit him at one point, which was evidenced by the tiny trickle of blood on Kyle's lip that I noticed when they took breaks to gasp for air.

I was holding myself together until I saw the pity flash across Ashley's and Layla's faces. They seemed to already have been aware of Kyle's conflicting behaviors, but had kept it to themselves out of loyalty to their boyfriends. Before I ended up soaking the entire dance floor in puddles of my own tears, I disappeared into the crowd in search of the nearest bathroom. Fortunately, there was no line, and I darted for an empty stall. I fully expected to bawl my eyes out under the cover of the loud music, but there were no tears left to cry. I had already used them all this afternoon, and the only feeling left was the pain of being humiliated.

Loneliness drowned me as I realized I was alone in a random Vegas bar's bathroom and would have to endure the hurt by myself, since I hadn't told Paige or Hannah where I had gone. In an effort not to alarm Ashley and Layla, who were probably planning on following me into the bathroom if I was gone long enough, I pulled myself together and exited the stall. My reflection looked like that of a girl who had just witnessed a tragedy and hadn't slept in days, but I made it my mission to reunite with the group and act as if Kyle's actions didn't bother me.

I eventually walked out and scanned the dance floor for the people I'd come with. It was crowded, but not enough to hide the tall Kingsley brothers. Out of the corner of my eye, I saw Layla dragging Mike out of the bar, with Ashley and Eli right beside them. Not too far behind was Kyle, who was drunkenly following them with his arm draped around the girl he had just met. It took me a second to realize that they were leaving the bar without me. I figured at least Ashley and Layla would have waited for me. Certainly not ditching a girl you'd arrived at a bar with was somewhere in the girl code. I tried to chase after them, but by the time I made it through the array of people, they were already gone. Panic settled in as I realized they didn't even care I wasn't with them. They probably hadn't even noticed I was gone.

I somberly exited the bar and dug into my purse to retrieve my pepper spray before starting the lonely walk in the dark back to my car. The guy who had invited me out couldn't have cared less where I was. He was too preoccupied with his blinding lust to even remember to check on me. I realized I had let my own self down by allowing my heart to be susceptible to this type of treatment again. Kyle Kingsley was nothing more than a lost man. I'd allowed him to break me down and build me back up with the building blocks of his own selfish desires.

As I retrieved my pepper spray, I noticed an object in my purse that didn't belong to me. I soon realized I was still in possession of Kyle's ID. I debated tossing it into the nearest dumpster, but as pathetic as it was, the reality that Kyle and I would have to see each other again was the silver lining to that terrible night.

12
Breakfast in Bed

On my way. Three words that without context meant so little. They barely held any weight and contained very few letters. The words were usually strung together to notify someone of your departure, but most didn't give them any more thought after that.

On my way. A phrase that didn't get the recognition it deserved until it was staring back at you in a message from a guy who'd just ditched you the night prior.

It didn't take long for Kyle to realize that his ID was missing, so I wasn't surprised when I woke up the following morning to his text asking if I still had it. What I wasn't prepared for was him immediately leaving his apartment once I sent him my unit number. He worked at the Exe on Sundays, but his shift didn't start for another four hours, so I wasn't sure why he was insisting on coming over so quickly.

On my way. Kyle Kingsley was on his way over to my apartment. I tried not to let my mind wander in the millions of directions this morning could go, but having him alone in my room provided endless scenarios.

Kyle's effect on me made me question my own emotions. On one hand, I hated how he treated me. He never consistently showed me grace and kindness without following it with a stab of hurt. His attention toward me was easily disturbed, and he could never keep his eyes off other girls. I hated that I couldn't trust him or predict how he was going to behave, but his cries for help were hard to ignore. Anyone could see that he held pain behind his eyes. I wanted to rescue him from his own self sabotage. I was good for him. I could fix the pain he carried in his heart. He had the power to change, and I wasn't ready to abandon him.

Kyle was in need of a girl to repair him, and I was up for the challenge.

Deep down, I knew it wasn't the smartest idea to see him again. I didn't know if it was his good looks and charming nature or my lonely heart, but the more he hurt me, the more I wanted to be around him. Kyle would always find a way to crush my hopes and play with my feelings to the point where I would feel so helpless that I would have no other choice but to run back to him. He caused me so much harm, but he was also the person who made me feel the most alive. Kyle was the hottest guy at the complex, and all the girls wanted him, yet he'd chosen me. I felt special. I felt desired. In a twisted way, I was kind of honored to be the girl he'd decided to play with, because at least when he was hurting me, he was giving me attention. Most would have said I deserved better than that, and I wholeheartedly agreed, but you accept the love you think you deserve, and that point in my life, I didn't even know if I was worthy of Kyle.

I changed out of my oversized T-shirt and into a more sensual pajama set made from a silky pink material that shimmered under the light. Paige had gifted it to me on my last birthday, but I had never actually worn it. I never felt the need to wear cute pajamas to bed when nobody else was going to see them, but today felt like the perfect opportunity. The material hugged my body just right and gave the impression that I slept like a princess. There were no drool marks or sweat stains on it, unlike my usual attire.

I redid my hair into a cute messy ponytail. It looked slept in, but not as wild as it had before. I sprayed myself with a light mist of perfume and added a dash of makeup to tie the entire Sleeping Beauty look together. Kyle would be unimpressed if he saw how I actually looked when I woke up.

Paige and Hannah were still asleep in Paige's bed, so I waited for Kyle in the living room. My plan was to drag him into my room as soon as he arrived, before Paige would have a chance to see him and lecture me about it. Kyle didn't know that she held a nasty grudge against him, and I was hoping to keep it that way. If he found out Paige didn't like him, he would realize that I had told her about all the mistakes he had made. I didn't want him to think I was talking negatively about him behind his back.

I knew that Kyle didn't live far, since I'd just been there yesterday, but his knock seemed to come quicker than the twenty-minute drive allowed. I panicked but stuck to my plan of letting him in quickly in order to hurry him into my room.

"Hey, Avery," Kyle blurted out when I opened the door. "Good to see you again."

He flashed a kindhearted smile at me, and it was hard to remember the anger I'd felt when I saw him ditching me for another girl. I knew I would have to confront him about it sooner rather than later, but I wanted a few more moments to enjoy this sweet version of him.

I successfully walked him back to my room without waking Paige and Hannah. He took a seat on the edge of my bed while I fetched my purse.

"I like your room," Kyle commented as he took in the minimalist decor.

Luckily, I had unpacked most of my boxes, so the space didn't seem like a total disaster, but there was still some work to be done.

"Thanks," I answered as I fished his ID from my purse.

The little plastic card that detailed Kyle's information was the sole thing holding our relationship together. If I hadn't been in possession of it, I wasn't sure we would've ever spoken again.

As I handed the ID back, Kyle decided to take the liberty of pulling me in for a kiss. It was a sudden gesture that caught me off guard. I enjoyed the brief moment, but I was quickly brought back to my senses when I saw the tiny scab on the top of his lip from the girl at the bar. She evidently had a strong bite.

"What's wrong?" he asked when he saw the sad look on my face.

"Um, well, you kinda left me at the bar last night," I hesitantly replied. "You forgot about me and then took another girl home with you."

I wished someone from the group had stopped to remember me, but I didn't hold the others responsible. I was Kyle's guest, and I'd expected more from him.

He stood up and started pacing around the room. This was another event that was pretty unforgettable to me but seemed difficult for him to remember. I knew he had been under the influence of a couple of drinks, but surely he recalled leaving with someone else.

"Oh, that girl." Kyle seemed to finally remember. "I sent her home as soon as she got back to my apartment. She was way too drunk."

My shoulders, which had been carrying the weight of all my pain and anger, felt slightly lighter after hearing that nothing had happened last night. I knew I should still be upset about the fact that he'd even entertained another girl, but his apologetic eyes were convincing me otherwise.

"Well, it wasn't fun watching you make out with her," I mentioned.

"Yeah, she even bit my lip," Kyle complained as he touched the healing cut.

He was clearly unaware that he had done anything wrong. The biggest issue in his eyes was the irritating wound. I contemplated expressing how much his actions had hurt me, but we weren't officially together, so I supposed he technically hadn't done anything wrong.

"It was kinda cute to see you jealous, though," Kyle whispered as he pulled me closer to him. "Makes me know that you really like me."

He planted a wet kiss on my forehead, and at that point I realized that there was no way I could stay mad at him. Of course he shouldn't have disrespected me by taking another girl home in front of my face, but at the end of the day, she'd been kicked out, and now he was in my bed. That was considered a win in my book.

I wasn't oblivious to the fact that he easily could've lied to me. It dawned on me that he was most likely lying right now and had probably hooked up with the random girl. I didn't want to imagine him being intimate with someone else. It pained me to even consider the possibility, so I just ignored it. Sometimes it's easier to just accept a lie than hear the truth.

The make-out session that I had blatantly refused last night because of the public setting was now being carried out in the privacy of my room. His weight on top of me felt like comforting armor shielding me from the worries of the world. I had Kyle Kingsley in my room all to myself, and nothing else mattered.

I woke up to the blaring sound of Kyle's alarm signaling that it was time to start his shift. After kissing until we ran out of breath, we had felt the presence of sleep creep up on us. Neither of us had fully recovered from staying out late last night, so we passed out in the comfort of my bed. When I'd woken up earlier this morning, I never thought that it would result in Kyle coming over and cuddling me until we fell asleep.

After last night, I hadn't even been sure we would ever speak again, but seeing him today restored all my faith in our growing relationship. It wouldn't be long before Kyle was officially mine. He was definitely one of the hottest guys I had ever seen. The mere sight of him gave me butterflies, but I think it was the conquest that really motivated me to want to be his girlfriend. I supposed I gave his opinion of me so much weight because of all the attention he commanded from women, but if I couldn't even get the pool security guard to date me, then who would?

Kyle groaned at the sound of the alarm. He rolled over but didn't make any effort to actually leave the bed. I wasn't complaining. If he wanted to stay for the rest of the day, I wasn't going to be the one to stop him. He performed a few more groans and stretches before finally gathering the strength to head off to his shift.

"When can I see you again?" Kyle yawned as he sat up and rubbed the sleep out of his eyes.

"Whenever you want," I said, and giggled. "You know where I live."

I wrapped my arms around him and nestled my head against his shoulder. I didn't want this moment to end, but I knew he had to leave for work. Even if I went up to the pool to see him, it wouldn't be the same as when we were alone.

"Let me take you on a date tonight," Kyle suggested. "I'll be back here at eight."

I internally leaped at the idea of going on a proper date with him. I hadn't thought the day could get any better, but he'd officially disproved that notion.

"I'll be ready." I beamed.

Kyle gave me one last kiss on the cheek before heading out. He gathered his things and exited my room as if he hadn't just given me the best morning of my life. I smiled at my ceiling, knowing that this was just the beginning of our love story. There was so much more in store for us, and I couldn't wait to see him again.

"What do you think you're doing here?" I heard Paige scream from the kitchen.

Crap. It seemed she wasn't working today.

"I was just grabbing my ID from Avery," Kyle responded hesitantly. "I gave it to her last night, and she held on to it for me."

There went my award-winning performance. I was supposed to be sick in bed over spoiled milk, and now there was a guy exiting my room in the early afternoon claiming to have been with me the night prior.

"Well, get out," I heard Paige threaten.

"Are you always this angry, or is it that time of the month?" Kyle returned.

I quickly jumped out of bed and raced toward the kitchen. He had poked the wrong bear, and I wasn't ready for a world war to break out in my apartment.

Paige, Hannah, and Kyle all turned in my direction when they saw me emerge from my room. I decided to handle one issue at a time, and my first mission was to get Kyle safely out of the apartment.

"You're welcome for the ID," I casually inserted as I headed straight for the front door. I hastily opened it as a signal for him to leave. He fortunately understood the hint and made his way out, but not before making the situation even worse.

"I'll be back tonight for our date," he said as he kissed me. "Don't forget."

He shot Paige a look, daring her to say something. She simply scoffed and turned away. Now there was definitely no chance that Kyle would ever be on her good side. Once he was finally out of sight, I shut the door behind him and got ready to embrace the wrath of Paige Jensen.

"I guess you made a speedy recovery," she sarcastically remarked as soon as the door closed.

"I'm sorry," I pleaded. "I didn't want to tell you because I know you don't like him."

"And do you know why I don't like him, Avery Kline?" she hissed.

As Paige and I sparred, Hannah stared speechlessly at us. Her head moved back and forth between us like a ping-pong ball. I felt bad that she was watching us argue, but I knew the worst was yet to come.

"Well, I'll tell you why," Paige continued when I didn't answer her. "Because he's rude, he has no respect for women, and he constantly hurts you. He has disrespected you to your face, discredited your feelings, and has never once treated you how you deserve. And who knows what he did last night? Based on his inconsiderate self, he probably kissed another girl in front of you! I have constantly tried to protect you, but if you won't defend your own heart, Avery, then who will? That man does not want you. He dangles the potential of a relationship in your face to keep you around, but in all reality, you're just another trophy on his shelf. I've told you multiple times that you are going to have to end this on your own, because men always come back. Kyle will always come back to you—not because he likes you, Avery, but because he's trying to see if you're still stupid enough to take him back."

Hannah's jaw almost hit the ground after hearing Paige's speech. She must have been unaware Paige was capable of crafting such words. There was a fly buzzing around the kitchen that I was afraid was going to make a home in Hannah's open mouth. However, I didn't stay long enough to find out. Before Paige could even finish her last sentence, I had already slammed my door in her face. She could make Kyle out to be the villain all she wanted, but the truth was, the only evil person in this scenario was Paige.

13
Change Is Inevitable

Kyle was late. Two hours late. I figured it was because it was taking him a while to get ready, but when he showed up at my door in his security uniform, it was evident that he'd never even left the complex. Our table at the restaurant had most likely been given to another couple by now, although they definitely wouldn't have seated us anyway, given Kyle's current attire. At least his sweatpants matched my tiny black dress.

"Ready?" Kyle asked, as if he was on time.

"Born ready," I returned, forcing a smile.

I grabbed my keys and shut the door behind us. Paige was home, but she stayed in her room since she refused to be in the presence of Kyle again. We weren't on speaking terms anyway, so it was probably for the best.

The last time I'd gone out with Kyle outside of the Exe Apartments, it had ended in a disaster. It was hard to shake the feeling that this night could end up being similar or even worse. He was incredibly unpredictable, and I wasn't sure which version of him was going to show up today. My nerves must've transferred to my hands, because when I tried to lock the door behind me, I ended up accidentally dropping my keys. They hit the floor with a jiggling clank that echoed throughout the hallways.

"Let me grab those for you," Kyle insisted.

He turned around and bent over to get them. As he reached down, his shirt slightly lifted, exposing his backside, and I noticed that his underwear was inside out. In that moment, I realized I didn't want to know what Kyle had been doing those two hours after his shift ended. He could have put them on the wrong way this morning. Still, knowing the type of guy he was, it was most likely the result of hastily throwing them on after being with a woman in order to quickly rush to a date with a different woman that he was extremely late for.

"Here you go." Kyle beamed as he handed me back the keys.

I took them out of his hand and locked the door behind me. The rush of excitement I had felt earlier was now replaced by a dreadful gut feeling. I was starting to think the version of Kyle that I held on to in my heart didn't exist.

We exited the apartment complex and headed in the direction of Kyle's car. The night sky was illuminated by the brightness of the stars. In the far distance, I could see a shooting star racing through the universe. When it got closer, I realized it was just a plane, but I took my chances anyway and made a wish. I was banking on a commercial aircraft to make my dream of Kyle turning into a gentleman come true.

"Do you think the restaurant canceled our reservation?" I asked, trying to make small talk.

"What reservation?" Kyle asked.

It was clear that he hadn't planned the date after he asked me out. I didn't want to jump to conclusions, as it was possible that he was about to surprise me and take me to a fancy restaurant that only locals knew about, but unfortunately, we ended up passing his car and walking straight into the run-down pizza shop next to the Exe. It reeked of stale bread and grease, and my tiny black dress clearly exceeded the dress code. I tried to hide my disappointment and continued to remind myself that Kyle wasn't used to taking girls on proper dates yet. He was trying his best, and I should be grateful for that.

"Can I get one large cheese pizza?" Kyle said.

He looked down at me and I nodded to confirm that I was satisfied with his order. I personally preferred pepperoni, but I liked that he'd taken charge and made a decision for us. He pulled out his wallet and handed over a ten-dollar bill.

"Sixteen dollars and ninety-nine cents," the cashier returned.

Kyle didn't look amused. He raised an eyebrow and scratched the back of his neck in his usual nervous response. "It's supposed to be half-off after ten," he asserted.

"Sorry bud, not on weekends," the man behind the counter said, pointing to the sign that listed terms and conditions of the discount, which clearly stated that the promotion was for weekdays only.

Kyle fished around in his wallet for more cash. He searched inside and out until he finally accepted that the money wasn't going to magically appear.

"I'm actually not that hungry," he said. "Can we get a medium instead?"

"Twelve dollars and ninety-nine cents," the cashier casually read off the register.

It didn't take a math wizard to realize that Kyle's ten dollars was still not enough to cover the bill. He frantically searched his wallet and pockets again, until I couldn't take the awkwardness of the situation anymore.

"It's fine. I got it," I said as I handed my credit card across the counter.

"Actually, on second thought, can we get an extra-large then?" Kyle quickly inserted. He scanned the menu one last time to make sure that he didn't want anything else. "Your dad gave you $25,000, right?" he reminded me.

I was a little uncomfortable paying on our first date. Even though I'd lied about the funds my father had given me, I didn't like the fact that Kyle was bringing up the money. It seemed to ease his guilt about not having enough money, because he didn't seem to care at all that I was picking up the tab. He was under the impression that we were using my dad's money to pay.

We found a booth in the corner of the pizza shop and claimed it as ours while we waited for the extra-large pizza. I was excited for the uninterrupted time with Kyle, but he was too distracted by his phone to make conversation. He looked up a few times to smile at me, but didn't say a word. He didn't even thank me for dinner. I figured he was just hungry and would return to his charming ways once he had some food in him. To pass the time, I decided to admire the handsome man sitting across from me. I stared at him under the flickering pizza parlor lights, but the inked serpent that was always wrapped around his left forearm shot me evil glances. I wouldn't have been surprised if the tattoo came to life once the sun went down, seeing as it loved to lure me into the temptation of its eyes at night.

Our pizza arrived ten minutes later, prompting Kyle to take his elbows off the table, relieving me from the pressures of the snake and ultimately forcing Kyle to put away his phone. The dinner continued in silence as we were busy eating, but I was hoping that the plane I had wished on earlier would eventually grant me Kyle's kindness sooner rather than later.

The pizza was good, but it was way too big for two people. There was over half of it left when Kyle and I had eaten more than our fill. I wasn't sure why he'd insisted on ordering the extra-large. I thought the medium would have been just fine.

We sat in our fullness for a while before engaging in conversation. When I saw he was about to speak, I let out a sigh of relief. I knew we weren't going to endure an entire dinner together without discussing the ins and outs of our relationship. This was the perfect opportunity to really get to know each other and talk about what we envisioned for our future.

"Can I take home the leftovers?" Kyle asked.

It seemed he wasn't as interested in talking about us as I was. I wasn't really sure what the purpose of this date had been. At least he'd gotten a free pizza out of it.

"Yeah, sure," I agreed.

Kyle closed the pizza box and stood up, indicating that it was time to leave. At least his car was parked at the Exe, so he was forced to walk me home.

I followed him back to the apartment complex in silence. It definitely wasn't the best date I'd ever been on, but at least nothing had gone seriously wrong. He hadn't kissed another girl in front of me or left me to walk home in the dark by myself. I'd heard that healthy relationships were sometimes boring because there weren't any toxic situations to fight over. Maybe that was the case here.

When we got to Kyle's car, he unlocked it and threw the leftover pizza in the passenger seat. I patiently waited for an awkward goodbye to end the night, but instead I was swept off my feet by a muscular arm. Kyle had swallowed my body in an overbearing hug and was blanketing my face with kisses. I would have preferred this amount of affection throughout the entire date, but my wish on an airplane had been granted, just after a little delay. Typical airline behavior.

"I had an amazing time with you," Kyle whispered as I giggled in his arms.

The midnight sky was painting the world around us in a gulf of darkness, but his eyes twinkled under the moonlit sky. The universe was still, and the only sound interrupting the deafening silence was our promising laughter. Although he had released me from his enamored hug, he was still gripping my hips, refusing to let me or this moment pass. His sweet side was emerging from the shadows, and the way he gently tucked my hair behind my ears sent me spiraling.

"Why don't we head back to your place?" Kyle winked as he nodded in the direction of my apartment. "I don't want this night to end."

An instant later, he and I were racing back to my room. I fumbled the key when trying to unlock the front door, but this time it was due to the excitement rather than nerves. Thankfully, Paige was not in the living room when we arrived. Kyle and I quietly inched our way to my room and dove onto my bed in a fit of kisses. There was a lot of built-up emotion from the night, and we were releasing all of the tension. Kyle intently felt his way to the top of my back and slowly began unzipping my dress. I tugged at his arm, showing that I wasn't interested in taking this any further, but he continued to pull at the zipper.

"What are you doing?" I breathlessly asked.

I loved our physical connection, but I wasn't ready to take it to the next level. It was too soon, and at this point, Kyle did not deserve anything more than a few kisses.

"Well, I gave you what you wanted," Kyle argued, "so I thought you were going to return the favor and give me what I wanted."

I pulled away from him in hysteric confusion. "What are you talking about?" I raged.

"You wanted something serious, so I took you on a date," Kyle pointed out. "Now I want something casual."

I continued to stare at him, confused and speechless.

"What?" Kyle asked. "I said I don't date residents, but I didn't say anything about hooking up with them."

He lunged for my zipper again, and this time, in an instantaneous reaction, I slapped him across the face. My hand made direct contact with his stubbly cheek in a stinging smack. Kyle jolted back with a look of surprise and rubbed his jaw. He couldn't believe that I had actually hit him, and honestly, neither could I. I shielded myself with a pillow in case of retaliation, but he didn't react. He quietly got up, removed himself from my room, and headed for the front door. Without saying another word, he left the apartment.

From the beginning, I had wondered what it would be like to officially go on a date with Kyle Kingsley, this legend of a man who secured the pool vicinity of the Exe Apartments. He had captured the hearts of all the bachelorette residents with his good looks and irresistible charm. It was known that Kyle would never succumb to the temptation of a resident, but somehow, I'd managed to weasel my way into the darkest depths of his heart. It was a place that no Exe resident had ever been before, and it certainly hadn't been occupied by anyone in a while. It was filled with cobwebs of pain and insecurity and dusted with the lies and hurts of past loves.

I'd tried to make myself a home in his defensive heart, but was met with abrupt resistance. Kyle had withstood all of my attempts to try to change his hardened outlook on love, and I returned with no results. Was it his fault for being so stubborn, or was I in the wrong for trying? Was I delusional for thinking that what I had to offer was enough? Was I crazy to believe that someone would actually want to better themselves in order to keep me in their life?

I had come to the conclusion that no matter what I did, I would never be able to change how Kyle treated me. It was not my responsibility to convince him of the good within me, but it was my duty to myself to not allow his actions to change me. I couldn't let one man's arrogance alter who I was inside. I refused to allow anyone else to dictate how I felt about myself. So no matter how hard I tried, I'd never be able to convince Kyle that I was worthy of a committed relationship. No matter how much effort I put into showing him how great I was, I couldn't change him…but he sure as hell couldn't change me either.

14
Picture Perfect

Mondays always sucked, but this one was extra awful. My best friend wasn't talking to me, Kyle and I were done, and my boss had given me until the end of the day to complete one of the most important assignments I'd ever had on behalf of the business. It was that time of year when every modeling agency in the country submitted one photo to the *Model America Magazine* in order to compete for the title of Modeling Agency of the Year. Ace had never won, but my supervisor was putting a lot of pressure on me to choose the right photo to bring the title to our company. Apparently, the executives thought we had a good chance this year.

Since I was the social media manager, I'd spent a lot of time researching other agencies, which landed me the responsibility of submitting the picture. I had one day to find a photo that fully represented our brand in the most positive light. Considering that my usual task was deleting negative comments off our social media pages, I wasn't as enthusiastic about the contest as the rest of the agency was.

I scoured through our entire portfolio, scanned every post, and searched through every photo shoot we had ever done. There was not a single image that jumped out at me. They were all flat, boring, and forgettable. Our stylist was clearly inspired by '60s makeup, because the eye shadow was the only thing on the models that stood out. The same poses were being replicated for each campaign, and we'd even recycled some of the same outfits. I wasn't sure why people thought we had a chance at winning the award, but they were probably the same ones who'd developed our marketing shoots and styled the models.

After several hours of trying to narrow down the pool of images, I decided to take a break to meet Hannah for lunch. It was Paige's birthday on Thursday, and we wanted to plan a celebration for her. We still weren't on speaking terms, but I wasn't going to let that get in the way of my best friend's special day. I shut my laptop, grabbed my purse, and headed toward the front door. When I walked through the living room, I saw Paige sitting on the couch playing with Toby and Leo. She glanced up at me, and we looked at each other in an awkward stare.

"Where are you going?" she asked distantly.

I could tell from her tone that she was still upset with me, but her effort to start a conversation was an attempt to extend an olive branch. This was the longest we had gone without talking in a while, and we were both ready for a truce. As much as I wanted to put an end to the fighting, I couldn't tell her the truth about where I was going. Hannah and I wanted our plans to be a surprise, and if I told her I was on my way to meet Hannah, Paige would offer to join. In an effort not to raise suspicions, I fed her the only excuse I knew she would accept without asking any further questions.

"Going to see Kyle," I answered.

The lie hurt my heart. I hated lying to my best friend, but I hated it even more because it involved me claiming to be hanging out with a guy who had no sense of boundaries. The mere mention of Kyle's name almost made me throw up in my mouth. He and I were never going to be friends again, but I couldn't let Paige know that yet.

She rolled her eyes at me and refused to continue the conversation. Her offer to reconcile had been retracted, and she went back to playing with Toby and Leo, completely ignoring my presence. Our fight would have to last a little bit longer, just until Hannah and I were finished planning her birthday. It was a little disheartening not to hear Paige's usual reminder to grab my keys before I left, but I slid them into my purse and locked the door behind me.

The drive to meet Hannah was filled with a guilty silence as thoughts about the status of my friendship with Paige swirled through my head. I couldn't wait until our argument was over. I missed her a lot.

"Are you ready to plan the best birthday ever?" Hannah asked when I finally arrived.

It had taken me a while to find parking, so I was a little late, but she accepted my apology and was eager to start brainstorming. I took a seat across from her and pulled out my phone to read the notes of ideas I had crafted. Unfortunately, all of the extravagant plans I had come up with were limited by either our budget or the lack of people that we knew were friends with Paige in Vegas. I realized she had her own social circle outside of Hannah and me, but I didn't know them, and I definitely didn't have a way to contact them.

"Why don't we just do a birthday dinner with the three of us?" Hannah suggested. "I know a cat-themed café that's not too far away!"

I was glad I'd included her in the planning session. Paige would love nothing more than to be around her best friends, food, and cats on her birthday.

"That's perfect!" I agreed. "I could also invite her brother, Graham. He lives back in Michigan, but I'm sure he wouldn't turn down a trip to Vegas."

It had been a while since I had seen Graham. In high school, I would come over to their house almost every day, but by the time I moved in with the Jensens my senior year, he had already gone off to college out of state. I'd always thought Graham was cute, and I even had a mini crush on him my last year of high school, but I think I just liked the fact that he was off-limits to me. Paige didn't approve of any of Graham's girlfriends, and we spent a lot of time in the cafeteria plotting their demises. She was the younger of the two, but she was very protective of her older brother. Everyone always wondered why Graham never seemed to be able to keep a relationship for long, but I knew there was a mischievous sister behind every breakup.

During our senior year, Paige finally matured and stopped caring about who Graham was dating, but I, on the other hand, took an even greater interest in his love life. I was developing feelings for him, and I loved hanging out with him whenever he would visit from college, but his relationships were getting in the way of our time together. He would bring girls home for the holidays and forget Paige and I even existed. Instead of taking us to get ice cream on the weekends, he would spend them snuggled up on the couch with his new girlfriend. I was slowly filling with envy, while Paige didn't even bat an eye. She wouldn't even throw an insult or uncomfortable comment in her brother's direction when they would kiss in front of us.

Without my partner in crime by my side, I had to come up with vengeance plans on my own. I wasn't as sharp as Paige in the realm of evil mastery, but I managed to break up the only serious relationship Graham ever had. All of his girlfriends until that point had been minor flings that lasted less than a year. Paige was the culprit of petty crimes, but I went for the felony.

Graham had met Sarah during his first semester of college. From the eavesdropping I had done on his conversations with Paige, I'd learned that he'd apparently rescued her from a vicious dog. Graham never mentioned the breed, but knowing the type of girl Sarah was, it had most likely been a Chihuahua. They'd been inseparable ever since.

Sarah was the type of girl that would change her outfit based on the time of day. She always had to look picture-perfect, and she was the world's biggest germophobe. If someone breathed too close to her, she would shower until she'd scrubbed off the top layer of skin. Her fear of microbes was irrational, but it provided me with the perfect opportunity to ruin her and Graham's relationship.

One summer when Graham was home from college with Sarah, Paige and I accompanied them to a country music festival. I was wearing a super cute denim jacket with a cowboy hat that Graham had gifted me for my fifteenth birthday, but his mouth was constantly locked with Sarah's that he didn't even notice. At one point during the day, the Jensen siblings had gone to find some food, leaving Sarah and me alone in the line for the portable restrooms. She must've really had to go, because her germ alert was going off, but she still stayed in line.

When she swallowed her fear for the few minutes it would take her to use the bathroom, I found a giant gentleman who was willing to accept a twenty-dollar bill in exchange for tipping over the portable toilet she was in. Needless to say, it was my best idea ever. Sarah let out a horrifying shriek as she was drenched in a horrendous-smelling liquid. She eventually managed to escape, and Paige and Graham returned to find her walking around like a swamp monster. With only me, Paige, and Graham around, it was clear that only one person in our group had the required strength to commit the crime. Once Sarah collected herself, she broke up with him on the spot and eventually fell in love with the emergency room doctor who tended to her "injuries."

Graham was a wreck for months after their split and spent even less time with me. I realized my plan had backfired when he returned to college with a broken heart and without falling in love with me. My feelings for him eventually faded, and I ended up going to a different college than him, where I dated my now ex-boyfriend, Ethan Wiley. I supposed Graham could be partly blamed for that toxic relationship, since I would never have been with Ethan if Graham had come to his senses and dated me, but either way, I was excited for the potential to see him again.

Hannah and I went our separate ways after our successful lunch date. I sent Graham a quick text inviting him to Paige's birthday before driving off to face my best friend, who was probably still on the living room couch hating my guts. I hadn't been gone long, but when I got home, it was obvious that Paige had already left to go nanny at the Thompsons' house. I walked in without needing to use my key. She had forgotten hers again, and our door was unlocked. I'd swear she'd never remember to grab a key, even if it was taped to her hand.

After my long break from work, I figured I would be rejuvenated enough to select the photo to submit to the *Modeling America Magazine*. I opened my laptop and went through the pictures I had already seen a million times. Their lack of unique styling and overused poses continued to bore me. I managed to complete a few more hours of aimless scrolling before I dozed off with my laptop still in my hands. Our portfolio was so useless that it literally put me to sleep.

My initial plan was to just rest my eyes and give my mind a break from looking through endless images, but I ended up passing out for the entire day. When I eventually awoke to the sound of my phone buzzing, the bright sun that had been shining through my windows when I began my nap was now hiding behind the mountains. I looked at my screen—a text from Graham.

I'm down! See you Thursday!

I was happy that he was coming for Paige's birthday. We had grown apart over the years and hadn't talked much. The feelings I'd had for him when I was younger never returned, and I was pretty sure he had a girlfriend now, but I was still excited to see him.

Figuring I had nothing better to do than confirm my suspicions about his relationship status, I took a quick glance through his social media accounts, but didn't find a single trace of a potential lover. There were only pictures of meticulously crafted meals, which I assumed he had prepared. He'd always loved to cook. A tiny butterfly fluttered in my stomach, and I wondered why I felt a little excited knowing that Graham was most likely single. I was still very much heartbroken over Kyle, and I was pretty certain that the last thing Graham would ever consider doing was dating his little sister's best friend.

I was abruptly snapped out of my thoughts when I realized the day was over and I still hadn't submitted a photo for the agency contest. I quickly opened my phone, found the picture of Paige, Hannah, and me in our matching red bikinis, and submitted it. We actually looked really hot in the photo, and it was more interesting than any of the ones that the agency had. My managers should actually be thanking me for not showing the judges anything we had in our boring portfolios. As much as they were relying on me to represent the company, there were more important things to think about than a stupid competition. Besides, I didn't like my job anyway. It would probably be a blessing if they fired me. I'd rather spend my night dreaming about my best friend's brother anyway.

15
Team Bride

Hannah was great at a lot of things. She was a wonderful cat mom, a brilliant dancer, and a genius birthday planner. She always had the most flawless skin and perfectly applied makeup. Her eye for cosmetics was second only to Paige Jensen's. She excelled at making people laugh and was an expert in entertaining a crowd. She possessed a handful of skills that would amaze anyone who got to know her. However, as talented as Hannah was, she was not great at hosting interventions.

I already knew something was up when she texted me to meet her in my own living room. It was a random Wednesday night, and we didn't have plans to hang out. Hannah would sometimes message me when she was bored or wanted to see if her cat, Tubs, could come over, but she specifically reserved Wednesdays for cleaning her apartment. Therefore, she had plenty to do.

I figured she might want to iron out any additional planning details or discuss Graham's arrival, but we had already solidified our plans for Paige's birthday dinner tomorrow, and Graham's flight was still predicted to land on time. There was nothing else I could think of that needed to be dealt with on a weekday night. I considered ignoring her text, but against my better judgment, I threw on my favorite East Tawas High School hoodie and opened my door to meet her.

I should have turned around right when I entered the living room, because when I walked out, I saw her sitting in a chair facing the couch with a stern look. She looked as though she were the principal of a high-achieving boarding school and I was the delinquent student who'd been called into her office for poor performance. I toyed with the idea of asking about the purpose of her authoritative presence in my living room, but when I saw Paige, I quickly realized where the situation was headed.

Paige was sitting in the left corner of the couch. She continued to ignore my presence and didn't even turn her head to look at me when I passed her. The right side was evidently reserved for me, and I hesitantly walked over and took a seat. Amazingly, Hannah had managed to lure both of us out of our rooms at the same time. I made a mental note to add "scheming" to the list of her many talents.

"Now that both parties are here," Hannah proclaimed, "we may begin."

Paige and I still refused to look at each other, instead staring intently at Hannah. The living room fell silent as we waited for her to continue. The whole charade seemed a bit extravagant. It had been almost a week since we'd been on speaking terms, but this was unnecessary. We would have made up on our own eventually. However, Paige's birthday was tomorrow, and we still hadn't forgiven each other. It would have been awkward to gift her the new kitten I had adopted for her if we still were fighting.

I'd rescued the kitten from a nearby animal shelter. It had been abandoned for being the runt of the litter, and I was drawn to its tiny size and life story. The kitten's eyes perfectly resembled Paige's, so I knew it was meant to be. Hannah had been more than happy to let the fluffy creature stay at her place until Thursday. She constantly sent me pictures of it, and I was afraid she was going to grow too attached and refuse to let me give it to Paige.

"I think it's time for you to be friends again," Hannah began. "I love both of you, and it's uncomfortable to watch you be mad at each other. Let's just hug it out and move on."

She ended with a hopeful smile and waited for either Paige or me to initiate the embrace. Unfortunately, her words were not as influential as she had hoped. I looked at Paige out of the corner of my eye, but she didn't budge. It was hard to stay mad at her, but I too did not move a muscle. I felt too much pride to be the one to break the stalemate. Even though Kyle and I were over, Paige had not been very supportive and had made multiple nasty comments about him. She could be mad at me all she wanted, but I had good reasons to be upset with her as well.

Sensing the lack of movement from either of us, Hannah decided to switch gears. Instead of using her soft, sweet tone, she found a demanding, persuasive voice from deep within her. I hadn't known she had a confrontational side, but her urgency to get us to make up had brought it out.

"If neither of you apologizes, then I'm canceling the birthday plans that Avery and I have been sneaking around to make," Hannah blurted out.

Her outburst caught Paige's attention. I could sense that this new information had shaken the grudge she was holding. In my peripheral vision, I could see her slowly turn her head toward me. I mirrored her movements, and we found each other making eye contact for the first time in days.

"You weren't actually hanging out with Kyle the other day?" Paige asked optimistically.

My hopes were quickly dashed as I realized this conversation was heading in the wrong direction. I was annoyed that she cared more about whether I had been around Kyle than the fact that Hannah and I had planned out her entire birthday, but I figured this would be the perfect opportunity to admit the half truth about what had happened between Kyle and me. If Paige had known the exact details of how far he had gone the night he came over, she would've had him fired or arrested. He was truly a pig, but he didn't deserve to lose his job or go to jail over it.

"We aren't going to be hanging out anymore," I admitted. "I finally decided to take your advice and leave him alone."

Paige's face lit up. She really was more focused on Kyle's and my relationship than her own birthday, but I couldn't help but love the smile she was wearing. It was an expression I hadn't seen in days, and I thoroughly enjoyed it even if it was based on a partial truth. I really was leaving Kyle alone. We hadn't talked since the last time I saw him, but I wasn't sure if I'd actually chosen that path or if Kyle had forced it upon me.

"I'm so proud of you!" Paige beamed as she pulled me in for a hug.

"Don't celebrate yet," I joked sarcastically. "He might show up at our door one day and beg for me back."

Paige paused and stared me straight in the face. "Yeah, but next time, you will be strong enough to say no," she reassured me.

I pulled her back into my arms for the first time in what seemed like forever. Despite the Kyle situation, we were best friends again, and I was so happy to have her back in my life. It had been the worst few days ever not being able to vent and talk about life with her. I had resorted to whispering apologies into Toby's and Leo's ears, hoping that they would find a way to pass on the message to her.

"He wasn't even that cute," Paige inserted nonchalantly.

"Too soon, Paige. Too soon," I murmured.

Hannah joined our hug, and we concluded the intervention by listening to Paige's potential theories about tomorrow's plans. She wasn't even close to guessing correctly, but I couldn't blame her. I wouldn't have guessed eating a cat-themed cake at a cat-themed café while being gifted a new cat either. Most importantly, Graham would get to be there to witness it all.

"I'm sorry that you and Kyle didn't work out," Hannah said sincerely. "I had the ultimate Las Vegas bachelorette party all planned out." Leave it to Hannah to be the comic relief.

"Well, there's no time like the present," Paige admitted.

After giving each other silent looks, we all giggled in agreement that tonight we would be celebrating my bachelorette party.

"Team Bride!" Hannah shouted as we raced to Paige's closet to pick out our outfits.

Nobody had proposed to me, and I had no plans to commit myself to marriage anytime soon, but the idea of celebrating with my best friends felt like a fresh start. Kyle was out of the picture, Paige was back in my life, and Graham was landing in Vegas tomorrow. With all the trials and tribulations I had faced up to this point, I was glad that they'd led me to the moment where I got to see Paige and Hannah honor my fake engagement.

It didn't take long for the apartment to be covered in glitter and party decor. We ordered a pizza from the place that Kyle had taken me to on our date, and it tasted a lot better when it was being eaten in good company. It was also nice to have someone else cover the bill and not bring up my family's financial situation.

Paige blasted music throughout the unit, but the real entertainment came from me telling her and Hannah the story of my first date with Kyle. I still chose to leave out the part about him trying to get me out of my dress at the end of the night, but they got a great laugh out of the series of unfortunate events. To correctly tell the story, I had to mention the part where I had lied about my father giving me an envelope with twenty-five thousand in cash, but Paige and Hannah found that hilarious too.

We ended the night falling asleep to romantic movies in Paige's bed, but awoke to my midnight alarm signaling the start of Paige's birthday. Hannah and I gave her twenty-two birthday pinches in honor of her age, which were met with cheerful squeals. If this night was any indication of how tomorrow was going to go, then Paige was about to have the best birthday ever.

16
Make a Wish

"Are we there yet?" Paige complained behind her blindfold.

It had been Hannah's idea to cover the birthday girl's eyes on the drive over to the Cat Café. I didn't think it was all that necessary, considering Paige would not have recognized the destination based on the route anyway. I don't think she even knew the place existed, but nonetheless, it added to the excitement, so I was more than willing to drive through strange alleyways and unpaved back roads under Hannah's strict direction that I take a few wrong turns to further confuse Paige. My GPS rerouted us at least eight times, and our ETA tripled over the course of our journey. I think the only person Hannah was actually confusing with her wild directions was me.

Last year for Paige's birthday, I'd surprised her with her own photo shoot. I saved up a few of the checks that my father had sent me over the months and hired an entire glam squad, professional stylist, and photographer to bring the entire vision to life. Paige was able to creatively direct the whole shoot. It was amazing to watch her thrive in her element and capture her love of fashion into a photo. I was always reminded of how grateful she'd been for the birthday gift by the numerous photos she'd hung up from the session. Every time she walked by one of them, she would pause to revel in the blissful memory.

I'd vowed to myself that I would keep trying to outdo each previous year's birthday until my brain could no longer fathom anything greater. Seeing the look on Paige's face year after year made it all worth it. This time, I'd used most of my dad's lottery money to cover the costs of moving to Nevada, but thankfully, Hannah paid for most of the decorations, and the animal shelter had practically given me the abandoned kitten for free. Graham covered his travel expenses on his own, and Hannah and I split the cost of the cake. Despite my financial situation and recent move, I wholeheartedly believed that this birthday would top last year's. Even a fashionista like Paige would choose a new kitten, her brother, and a cat-themed restaurant over a photo shoot.

Before Hannah and I had left the apartment with Paige, Graham texted me to let me know that he had landed. Once he'd collected his luggage and picked up the rental car, he was going to meet us for dinner. Hannah and I would have to stall Paige for a few minutes before he arrived, but we were experts in distraction. I couldn't wait to see the look on her face when her brother finally walked in, but I was even more excited to see how he had aged over time. He'd always possessed stunning features, but hid them behind his shyness. His sister and mother were the more extroverted ones of the family, and Graham and his father seemed to thrive outside of the limelight.

After circling what seemed like the entire city of Las Vegas, I pulled into the parking lot of our destination. I wasn't sure if this dinner was more for Paige or Hannah, because Hannah was practically jumping out of her seat when we arrived. When I finally stopped in a spot right outside the entrance, she opened her door and ran out of the car, completely forgetting about Paige in the backseat. I had to carefully guide her out, since she was still blindfolded and my partner in crime had ditched me to pet a stray cat that I assumed belonged to the café. It was a beautiful feline with an orange coat that blended in perfectly with the desert environment. It didn't have a collar, but the way it lingered around the restaurant made it seem like this was its home. I slowly guided Paige toward the front door until Hannah was fully satisfied that she had endured enough blindness for the day.

"Okay, you can remove your blindfold!" she shouted excitedly, holding the stray cat in her arms.

Paige reluctantly removed the cloth from around her eyes. She blinked a few times to clear her vision before taking in her surroundings. It took her several moments to fully understand where we were, but the abundance of cat decor outside the café was pretty revealing.

"Is this heaven?" she said when it finally clicked. Her eyes danced around trying to find something to fixate on, but she found a joyful surprise in every direction.

"Almost!" Hannah exclaimed as she ushered us both inside.

She was still holding the parking lot cat and had brought it inside without hesitation. I was hoping it belonged to the owners or that they accepted animals, because Hannah showed no signs of letting it go. I knew this was a cat-themed establishment, but that didn't mean their health codes allowed felines.

When we entered the waiting area, I realized that I'd been mistaken in my judgment of Hannah's decision to bring the stray cat inside. Paige and I looked the most out of place not having one in our arms. There were so many cats roaming around the place that I couldn't tell if we were at a café or a shelter. A few of the customers had even brought their own pets to dine with them. For me, it felt overwhelming, unsanitary, and chaotic, but for Hannah and Paige, it was pure paradise.

"Reservation for Hannah Livingston," Hannah told the hostess. "We're here for a very special occasion."

Hannah turned to give Paige a giant wink, which she returned with an enthusiastic thumbs up. The hostess clearly knew about our birthday reservation, which Hannah had worked closely with the café to coordinate. Still, we continued to indulge in normal restaurant behavior in order to not alert Paige to all the surprises we had planned.

"Right this way."

The hostess guided us to the back, to the most overdecorated table that I had ever seen in my life. Hannah had gone all out with the décor, and I felt bad for my minuscule financial contribution. She had mentioned that she was only going to buy a couple of party favors, but evidently got carried away in the process. There were dozens of helium balloons that hovered around the area, rainbow confetti covering the entire table, and fun party hats to top off the celebration.

We sat down and took in the wonderful decorations. There were three curious cats circling around our table trying to join the party, and Paige took the liberty of picking one of them up to put in her lap. The table was set for four, so there was an empty chair next to me. I wondered if Paige had noticed the extra table setting, but she seemed too preoccupied with her new feline friend to notice.

"Happy birthday!" the waitress shouted in her direction. "Can I get you guys started with anything to drink?"

Hannah and I were satisfied with water, but Paige opted for her usual vanilla latte. When the waitress returned with her drink, it was topped off with whipped cream and sprinkles. Paige was in such awe that she was dining with her best friends, fifty cats, and a caffeinated beverage that she barely said a word. She was too busy indulging in the best birthday latte she'd ever had and contemplating which cat she was going to adopt. Little did she know that there was a cute little kitten waiting patiently at home for her.

"Can you take a picture of me?" Paige begged as she held three cats in her lap, with two more climbing on top of her. "I need to photograph this memory."

I was sitting across from her, so I pulled out my phone to capture the moment. Hannah leaned out of the view of my camera, but I was too close to get every single animal into the photo. Paige waited patiently as I scooted my chair back to get a wider shot. The cats were starting to get fussy, so I tried to move as quickly as possible to get as many as I could in the shot before they darted off. I grabbed the bottom of my seat and lifted it off the ground. Without looking, I forced it backward, but was met with solid resistance and a screeching yelp. I was too in shock to turn around, but from the groaning I heard behind me, I could tell I had rammed my chair into an innocent bystander. I saw Paige's eyes widen, so I figured I must have really caused some damage.

"Well, this wasn't the welcome I was expecting," my victim croaked.

"Graham!" Paige shouted as she flung the cats off her.

My cheeks flushed bright red from the rush of embarrassment, and I chose to refrain from showing my face until I'd returned to a normal color. I hadn't envisioned Graham's arrival involving me ramming into him, but at least he had made it to Paige's birthday dinner. I was excited that he was here, but it had been a while since I'd been around him. After this trip, I wasn't sure when I would see him again, and I didn't want the wooden remnants of my chair to be the only thing that stuck with him.

"I see you're still as clumsy as ever," Graham pointed out as he took the empty seat next to me.

I subtly felt my cheeks before facing him. They still felt a bit hot, but I figured most of the redness had probably subsided. I turned to fire back a witty comment, but my breath was cut short by the sight of him. My throat tightened and the air that had once filled the room seemed to have disappeared. My brain lapsed, and I couldn't formulate a single sentence or articulate a thought. Graham Jensen had stolen the world around me and centered it around him. His presence was unbearable.

He was more beautiful than I had remembered, and I didn't feel worthy enough to lay my eyes on him. His body had matured, and time had added another three inches to his height and another forty pounds of muscle. He possessed the typical Jensen features—light brown hair and hazel eyes—but his face contained a mixture of softness and maturity. His gaze seemed to communicate with me in an unspoken language, and I immediately felt a sense of safety around him. I had known him for so long that I was able to bask in the comfort of him, but at the same time, I was intrigued by the newness of him. He was a human masterpiece that not even the best artist in the world could have done justice.

"I'm Hannah Livingston," Hannah excitedly announced, interrupting my train of thought. "I live in the same apartment building as Paige and Avery."

Her interjection brought my floating soul down to earth. Graham and Hannah exchanged brief introductions before Paige started firing questions at us about how we'd been able to pull off such a surprise. This brief moment of freedom from the grip of Graham's attraction afforded me the precious time I needed to regain control over myself.

"It was all Avery's idea," Hannah confirmed. "Just wait until you see the gift she got for you. It's waiting for you in my room."

Hannah was proud of herself for not spoiling the kitten surprise up to this point, even though I could see her lips loosening up to tell. I was hoping that the present would remain a complete surprise until we got back to the apartment, but I couldn't blame her for her excitement. If Graham wasn't enough to set this birthday above last year's, the kitten definitely would be.

The waitress returned to take our food orders. The menu was full of extravagant dishes, but Hannah and I knew there was a giant cake ready to be devoured after we finished our dinner, so we chose lighter options. We tried to hint to Paige and Graham to follow suit, but Graham was not willing to comply.

"I haven't eaten all day," he insisted. "I'm not ordering a salad."

"Come on, Graham," I urged. "You'll want to save room for dessert."

I realized I had basically revealed that there was a birthday treat reserved for us, but I couldn't think of anything else to prevent him from ordering the entire menu.

"Are you implying that I can't eat a full meal and a dessert, Avery?" Graham asked. "Are you saying that I am getting fat?" He laughed and jokingly grabbed the sides of his stomach.

"What are you talking about? That is not what I was trying to say. You obviously have an amazing body," I said defensively.

Graham was in great shape. I could see the outline of his six-pack through his shirt, and his legs were challenging the seams of his pants. He was in possession of a perfect body, and his comment was simply a pathetic beg for a compliment. He'd always loved getting a reaction out of me and baiting me into saying things I didn't mean. It came with the territory of being his little sister's best friend. I usually just rolled my eyes at him, but it had been a while since I'd been the target of his mischievous ways, and I had mistakenly let my guard down.

"I meant to say that I want you to be hungry. Well, not hungry, but able to eat cake. I mean, you don't have to if you don't want to. Your body is fine, and you know what's best for it. I didn't mean fine as in average. It's better than fine. I mean, from what I have noticed. I wasn't looking that hard or anything—"

"He'll have a house salad," Paige interjected to the waitress, who was waiting on the last order. "Graham, stop giving her a hard time. She's had enough boy drama lately."

"Oh, Avery has a lover?" Graham asked, intrigued.

"Ex-lover," Hannah offered proudly.

I was starting to think inviting Graham to the birthday dinner had been a big mistake. Kyle Kingsley was the last thing I wanted to talk about, especially in front of him.

"Yeah, he is definitely not in the picture anymore. According to him, it's funny to pretend like Avery doesn't exist and then flirt with other girls in front of her," Paige said.

She continued to paint her villainized version of Kyle for Graham. She exaggerated some parts of the story, and I wanted to defend him after every incident she described, but her stories weren't as bad as the things she didn't know about, so I decided to keep my mouth shut. She slowed down when our food came, but still managed to express how terrible of a person he was as pieces of salad made a home in her teeth.

The cake being brought out was the only thing that put a stop to her rant. I was on the brink of tears when Paige finally finished bashing Kyle and decided to focus her attention on blowing out the candles. I didn't want to ruin her dinner, so I kept my emotions to myself, but her divulging the embarrassing treatment that I'd endured was very hurtful. Kyle had not been my finest choice, but I didn't want my business advertised to her brother.

I was soaking in my pity while Hannah and Paige took videos of all of the cats roaming around the restaurant. Before I could excuse myself to the bathroom to pull myself together, I felt a hand gently grab my thigh. I looked down and trailed my gaze up Graham's arm until I met his eyes.

"You know, I also dated someone crazy once," he whispered. "We went to a music festival together and she accused me of tipping over the portable toilet she was in. You wouldn't happen to know anything about that, would you?"

He flashed a sly smile. A rush of guilt shot through my body, and I sat straight up in my chair. I hadn't been prepared for an evil revenge plan from my childhood to be brought into the light. Of course I felt bad that I had interfered in Graham's personal life, but it was the only time that I had actually sabotaged any of his relationships. I thought I'd gotten away with it. All these years, I had triumphed in the glory of the belief that I had secretly forced Graham to be single again, but apparently he had known the entire time.

"I have no idea what you're talking about," I responded with a sarcastic tone, "but she sounds crazy."

I took a sip of my drink and bite of cake to suppress my guilty smile, but he was already chuckling, watching his sudden revelation cause chaos in my brain. Graham continued to comfort me by keeping his hand rested on my thigh. It felt so natural that I almost forgot we hadn't talked in months. Paige's birthday had been full of surprises, but Graham Jensen was the best one of them all.

17

The Bright Side

Living with a roommate who loved to indulge in lattes usually meant that there was never a shortage of milk in the refrigerator. Besides the recent incident where we'd had to throw out the expired gallon, I was never concerned about the amount of dairy in our apartment. Therefore, it never occurred to me to check our supply before I poured my cereal, but the carton in the fridge was empty. My Friday morning breakfast definitely could have used the missing ingredient. I refused to attempt to cook again, so I settled for cereal without the milk.

While I was chomping away on the dry, sugary bits, Graham awoke from his slumber on the sofa and made his way into the kitchen wearing only a white T-shirt and boxers. His hair was a tangled mess on top of his head, and he hadn't even been awake long enough to rub the crust out of his eyes. He appeared as though he had barely escaped a tornado, but still somehow looked even better than he had last night. He lazily stumbled into the kitchen searching for his next meal, but paused as he walked past me.

"You know, I actually have the fire department on speed dial if you decide that you want to try to make an actual breakfast," he joked.

I loved that Graham knew me so well, but it also meant that he knew all of my flaws. I'd tried to cook for him and his family a few times in the past, but I was pretty sure the Jensens had banned me from the kitchen after I melted over half of their cookware.

"I'm trying something different," I responded in attempt to hide my defeat. I continued to suffer through my dry cereal. Milk would have really helped.

"You still like your bacon crispy with sunny-side up eggs?" Graham asked as he grabbed some pans from the cabinet.

"Extra crispy," I said, and smiled.

Graham continued to collect everything he needed and proceeded to make a true breakfast. The sound of the bacon sizzling and the smell of fresh eggs cooking on the stove made me drool. The sight of real food made my stomach dance, but the view of Graham making it was what made my heart sing. If he was going to cook for me every morning, then he could stay as long as he wanted.

"Benny, no!" Paige shouted as she ran out of her room chasing her new kitten.

She was still trying to tame her latest birthday gift, who'd turned out to be a major troublemaker. Toby and Leo had always been low-maintenance pets. Even as kittens they were relatively calm. They wrestled every once in a while, but for the most part, they kept to themselves. Benny, on the other hand, was a furry hazard. The animal shelter had told me he'd been given up because of his small size, but I think they forgot to mention the part about him being quite the handful. He was a ball of energy, but I think Paige secretly loved the challenge.

"Toby, Leo, and Benny are having a playdate with Tubs later today if you want to join," Paige offered, clearly out of breath from chasing the kitten around. "We are hoping that the older cats will teach Benny how to behave."

Paige didn't have to nanny today, which gave her more time to get accustomed to the new cat.

"That's okay," I answered, still salivating over the bacon, eggs, and her brother. "I've got a lot of work to do today."

As much as I hated my job, hanging out with Hannah's and Paige's cats seemed like an even greater nightmare. When those two were around their pets, nothing else in the world mattered, and I didn't feel like having my Friday afternoon centered around cats.

"Maybe next time," I said politely.

Paige ran back into her room to chase after Benny right as a delicious plate of bacon and eggs were placed in front of me. They were still sizzling from the heat of the pan, and the savory aroma filled my nose. The eggs were cooked perfectly, and the glowing yellow yolks were begging to be devoured. My mouth watered over the delicious food and the handsome chef who'd made it.

"Breakfast is served," Graham exclaimed as he sat down next to me with his own plate. "Specially prepared by yours truly."

I couldn't help but laugh at the idea of Graham and me sitting down to breakfast together. We had done it plenty of times when we were younger, but this felt different. It felt right.

I immediately reached for a piece of bacon despite knowing that it was still extremely hot. My tongue burned from the hot grease, but my stomach was happier than ever. I shoved a few more pieces in my mouth before quickly switching over to the eggs. I lunged my fork straight into the center, and the yolk oozed all over my plate, covering it in a sea of yellow goodness. My food was rapidly disappearing off my plate, and I inhaled it as if I hadn't eaten in days. Out of the corner of my eye, I saw Graham staring at me, and I realized that for a second I had forgotten I was in the presence of company. I abruptly reined in my barbaric manners and reached for a napkin to dab the corners of my mouth, attempting to show a more proper side.

"What a mighty fine meal, I must say," I expressed in a formal tone. "Wouldn't you agree, Mr. Jensen?"

I used a fork and knife to carefully cut my next bite of bacon, as if it were a prime slab of steak. It seemed outrageous to eat bacon without my hands, but it was funny to go from scarfing down my food to properly consuming it.

"It is a very fine meal indeed, Ms. Kline," Graham agreed in an equally pretentious tone. He chose to mimic my actions and used a fork and knife to eat his bacon.

We continued our breakfast as if we were dining with royalty and periodically burst into fits of laughter. It was hard to keep a straight face watching such a large man eat so daintily. After a few minutes, my hunger took over, and I decided to ditch the silverware and use my hands again. Bacon was not something that should be eaten with utensils. Graham followed suit, seeming relieved to resume to his normal manners.

"So how'd you know it was me who tipped over the bathroom Sarah was in?" I blurted out through a mouthful of food. It was a random time to bring it up, but I hadn't been able to fall asleep last night wondering how he'd figured it out.

Graham choked slightly on his breakfast before answering. My question had apparently caught him off guard. "The guy you paid to push over the stall was a friend of mine," he explained. "He mentioned it to me about a month after the breakup."

I dropped my head in shame. Paige would definitely have been disappointed in my inability to execute my revenge plans without getting caught. I was simply not the evil mastermind that she was.

"I had a crush on you back then, and I was jealous of your relationship with Sarah," I admitted. I had never actually voiced my feelings for Graham before, and I was nervous to see how he would respond. "I'm sorry. I was young and dumb."

He scraped up the last of his eggs and finished the rest of his breakfast without saying a word. I wasn't sure if this meant he accepted my apology or that he was still mad at me. The tension between us grew, and the awkward silence was deafening. It was only when I couldn't take the uncomfortable situation any longer and checked my phone that I snapped back to reality, realizing I was late for a conference call with the executives. They had called an emergency meeting last night, and I assumed it was because they were going to announce that it would be my last day at Ace Modeling Agency. My managers had never liked the fact that I didn't have a passion for the industry like they did, and I was sure they'd wasted no time gossiping to their bosses about it. I was trying to find a new job anyway, so being fired wouldn't be the end of the world. I quickly grabbed my plate and stood up with a sense of urgency.

"Don't worry, Avery, I'll get the dishes. You're obviously late for something," Graham said quietly.

He sluggishly stood and removed all the dishes from the table, placing them in the sink. He still seemed to be in a somber mood, and I knew I couldn't go into my meeting without at least apologizing again.

"I'm really sorry about Sarah," I told him. "I shouldn't have gotten involved."

Graham was evidently still not over her. My careless actions had ruined a relationship that he was very passionate about. She was the only girl he'd dated seriously, and I'd potentially destroyed his only chance of ever finding a love like that. I cautiously turned to leave Paige's grieving brother behind and face my career fate.

"I'm not upset about Sarah," Graham blurted out right as I reached my room. "I'm upset that you claimed having a crush on me was young and dumb. I had a crush on you too, Avery, but it was the best feeling I ever had."

I blankly stared at him as the kitchen sink continued to run behind him. The sound of the water would have drowned out any response that I could have given him if I'd been able to formulate an answer. Instead, I abruptly left to join the executive meeting I was already late for.

They say good things come to those who wait. Apparently, good things also came to those who went behind their companies' backs. When I logged in to the meeting a few minutes late, it was clear that I had been holding up the start time, since I was met with rolling eyes when I joined. It was a little awkward to be the only remote employee, seeing as everyone else was gathered around a large table and I was attending virtually, but I was glad they hadn't made me fly all the way to New York to deliver the news. I was shocked by how many employees had been invited to join the call where I would be officially terminated, but I'd stopped being surprised by the company's actions a long time ago. The executives didn't seem to be bothered by my tardiness, but my managers were highly displeased. I figured it was my last day anyway, so I wasn't too concerned about their thinning patience.

Without wasting any more time, the chief executive officer, Oscar Downs, began by telling the group how amazing Ace Modeling Agency was. He expressed how great the organization was doing financially and how many upcoming photo shoots we had planned. Ace was also in the process of important contract negotiations, which would lead to collaborations that would further boost the brand. I figured if I was going to be fired, Oscar Downs wanted me to at least know what I was missing out on. He continued to brag about the company until he came to an unexpected pause and a sudden shift in topic.

"Now, let's get to the real reason why I called you all here," he said. "We all know that *Model America Magazine* has the privilege of awarding one company the Modeling Agency of the Year award. We have been so close every time but have never been honored with the prestigious title. Avery Kline was given the responsibility of submitting the entry on Ace's behalf this year and chose an interesting image."

Even though I was thousands of miles away, the CEO appeared to be making direct eye contact with me through my computer screen as he passed around the photo of me, Hannah, and Paige in our red bikinis. The picture was met with confusion, since it was clearly not one that belonged to the agency. Mr. Downs had obviously recognized me in it and decided that this would be the perfect opportunity to call me out in front of the entire team. Since I'd basically gone behind everyone's back and chosen a picture that wasn't in our portfolio, I actually didn't blame them for wanting to get rid of me. I probably would have fired myself.

"Together, we have been through many hurdles. We have worked so hard as a company to carefully craft photo shoots and hire models that perfectly exemplify who we are. I'm as surprised about the photo submission as you all are, but I am happy to announce that Ace Modeling Agency is this year's winner."

Oscar Downs' news was met with loud cheers and rounds of applause. I flashed a giant smile, even though I was hiding my racing heart. I was slightly bothered by the fact that I had single-handedly saved the future of the business that I was trying to leave, but at least I hadn't been publicly humiliated during the meeting.

To my surprise, and my managers' surprise, the executive committee of the agency collectively gave me praise for my deceitful action. Apparently, the photo I submitted had been met with overwhelmingly positive reviews and high marks from the judges. The magazine wanted the photo of me, Paige, and Hannah in our red swimsuits to be featured on the cover of next month's issue. Our company was overjoyed with the widespread publicity we were about to receive, but I think the executives were more thrilled about the large sum of money that came with the award.

The emergency meeting that I assumed was going to be my doom had turned out to be my best day on the job. After it was over, upper management had me stay on the call, and I received a promotion to director of marketing, accompanied by a generous salary bump. I was ecstatic at the title change, but like the executives, I was more impressed with the extra money that came along with it. My new paycheck was more than double what I used to get each month, and that was including the extra cash from the checks my father had sent. My financial situation had abruptly changed because of one hasty decision.

"Thank you for your services, Avery," Mr. Downs congratulated me as he concluded our meeting. "I look forward to your future at Ace Modeling Agency."

As soon as the call ended, I immediately ran to find Paige to give her credit for encouraging the matching bikinis and to celebrate my new role. I raced to her room and started frantically knocking on her door.

"You're not going to believe what just happened!" I exclaimed as the handle gradually turned. However, when it finally opened, my best friend wasn't standing there. Instead, I was looking at her gorgeous older brother, who had clearly just gotten out of the shower. Thousands of water droplets were scattered across his bare skin. He was only covered from the waist down by a flimsy towel that was not made to shield such a large man. A simple gust of wind would have revealed a lot more than I was ready to see, but I wouldn't have been too upset if a slight breeze made its way into the apartment.

"She already left for Hannah's," Graham said as he looked me up and down.

"I'll just wait until she gets back, then," I mumbled. I briefly debated running over to Hannah's unit, but I figured Benny was probably causing havoc by now.

"Well, what is she not going to believe just happened?" Graham asked, clearly interested in my news.

I giggled as I headed back to my room. "That her brother used to have a crush on me."

Graham seemed unamused by my joke and shut Paige's door before I had a chance to redeem myself, but between getting promoted and seeing him shirtless, I wasn't sure the day could get any better.

18
Craving S'More

"Why is the front door unlocked?" Graham asked when he returned from the gym. I had given him my key to let himself back in after his workout, but he hadn't needed it.

He threw his bag on the kitchen table, his musty fumes filling the air. His gray shirt was drenched in sweat, revealing the layer of muscle underneath. At this point, his clothes were just a tease, hinting at the body I had already seen yesterday.

"Your sister just left to nanny," I responded as I browsed the pantry for a snack. "She never remembers to lock it."

"Well, what if someone breaks in?" he asked as he examined the door.

"Yeah, and steals what?" I snickered. "Our priceless toaster?"

Graham ignored me and began looking around our apartment. He lifted up the living room rug, checked behind the couch pillows, and even opened our cookie jar. Every inch of the place was searched, as if he had lost something valuable.

"What are you looking for?" I exclaimed.

"I'm looking for the envelope of money your dad gave you," he said sarcastically, popping a cookie into his mouth.

I'd forgotten that the birthday dinner had consisted mostly of Paige spilling all the details of my relationship with Kyle, which included my little lie about my family riches. Graham must have figured that enough time had passed that he could now make fun of me for it. He continued to joke about my failed relationship until I eventually found a bag of marshmallows. Using his forehead for target practice, I tried to pelt him with the fluffy candies. Most of them ended up on the floor, which wasn't a deterrent for Graham, who picked them up and started eating them.

"What?" he moaned through his sticky mouth. "You don't like marshmallows?"

I looked at him with a mixture of disgust and adoration, because even with a cheekful of candy, he was still as handsome as ever.

"I don't," I replied, "but even if I did, I wouldn't eat them off a dirty floor."

He switched to grabbing candies out of the bag as he snacked on a few more.

"So how do you eat s'mores?" Graham gasped as if I had offended the entire marshmallow family.

"Just chocolate and graham crackers," I answered proudly.

Bonfires were a summer essential in Michigan. My friends always wondered how I made my s'mores, but I refused to eat them any other way. I loved the crunch of the cracker and sweetness of the chocolate, but had never understood the satisfaction of the marshmallow. It always stuck to the roof of my mouth and left a mess behind. I preferred desserts without a gluey texture.

"I'll be the Graham cracker to your s'mores," Graham said, then chuckled at his own pun.

His joke was super cheesy, but I played along anyway. "And I'll be the chocolate to yours."

"Now all we need is a marshmallow."

Graham slowly inched closer to me, and before I knew it, I was wrapped up in his arms while he was trying to force-feed me the gooey marshmallow that was melting in his warm hands. I struggled to escape his grip, but he was too strong, and I was out of breath from laughing so hard. I tried to fight him off a little longer, and he eventually decided to eat it himself. He successfully finished it, but made a giant mess in the process.

"It's all over your mouth," I pointed out, laughing and staring at the chaos on his face.

Graham's lips were covered in a sticky white residue. He tried to use his tongue to lick away the mess, but the marshmallow stayed glued to him. I lightly dampened a napkin to try to wipe away the rest of it myself, but his height made it difficult to properly help him. He noticed my struggle, so he lifted me onto the kitchen counter in one swift movement. Within seconds, we were eye-level with each other, and I couldn't remember if I had ever been this close to his face before. I could see the green and brown pigments in his eyes that gave them their hazel color. His freckles, which appeared faint from a distance, were very apparent close up. Each hair on his head was clearly defined, and I could see every wrinkle and crevice that made up his beautiful, majestic face.

"Are you sure you don't like marshmallows?" Graham whispered as he gently brought his lips closer to mine.

Even with us at the same level, his large frame still towered over me. His biceps were bulging as his hands squeezed the counter on either side of me. I could feel his warm breath on my lips, and it took all the power I had to refrain from kissing him.

"On second thought, I actually can't remember the last time I had one," I mumbled quietly against his mouth.

Graham took my answer as the green light he needed to make a move. He studied my lips before pulling me even closer to him. Our mouths met in a swarm of passion and stickiness. A rush of heat flooded my entire body, and butterflies filled every inch of my stomach. I'd thought the fireworks described by the characters in my romance movies were an exaggeration, but kissing Graham felt like the Fourth of July. I usually hated marshmallows, but this time, they were the best thing I had ever tasted.

Our lips were obsessed with each other, and I wasn't sure if they were stuck together by the candy or our urge for each other. It felt as though we couldn't get enough of one another, but we immediately separated when we heard the rustle of the front door. Graham was on the opposite side of the kitchen before Paige even fully opened it.

"Forgot my phone charger," she muttered when she ran past us.

Graham and I exchanged apprehensive looks as she disappeared into her room.

"I swear, Jensens never remember to lock doors," I said with a smile, hopping off the counter.

Graham breathed a sigh of relief. We weren't sure how Paige would react to us kissing, but we definitely weren't ready to find out.

"I'm never forgetting to lock a door ever again," he assured me as he reached for another handful of marshmallows.

The nights Paige was at the Thompsons' were usually the loneliest times of the week, but this time, her absence gave me the space I needed to make out with her brother. I tried to show him my favorite romantic comedy, but I wasn't sure how much of the movie we actually ended up watching. I had spent so much time inside Graham's mouth that the taste of his tongue was permanently imprinted on my taste buds. As much as my body craved him, I couldn't remember the last time we'd actually eaten. My stomach was shouting for food, but my mouth was preoccupied with other things.

"I'm getting hungry," I complained, staring into Graham's eyes as we finally took a break for air. He lazily gazed back at me, love-drunk on kisses.

"And what would you like to eat, Avery?" he inquired as he readjusted himself on the couch. He started playing with my hair with one hand while calling a pizza place with the other. His question seemed to be merely a formality, since he wasted no time in ordering an extra-pepperoni pizza from my favorite restaurant. I'd forgotten that he could basically read my mind. Graham finished placing the order and focused his attention back on me.

"Let me pay," I offered as I tried to remove myself from the couch to fetch my purse. "You're my guest."

I felt bad that I had asked Graham to travel so many miles from home just to have him end up paying for my dinner. He had already covered everyone's meal at Paige's birthday, and I didn't want him to continue buying other people's food. Between all the cooking and checks he had covered, it was time for him to be treated for once. I tried to get up, but he held on to my waist and refused to let me go find my credit card.

"You're not touching your wallet around me," Graham explained sharply.

"What are you talking about?" I stammered, his serious tone catching me off guard.

"I'm not sure who taught you how you're supposed to be treated, but you're not paying for anything," he clarified, kissing the side of my cheek.

I appreciated his pride in wanting to financially care for me, but I could never ask someone to do that. He must have sensed my apprehension, because he pulled me closer to him.

"Don't worry, Avery. I'm only trying to show you how you deserve to be treated," Graham said, "but if you truly feel the need to buy me something, like maybe a new set of golf clubs, I'm not going to stop you."

We laughed but ended up spending the next thirty minutes browsing the internet for the clubs he wanted. He had obviously been joking about me buying them for him, but I insisted that he at least show me which ones he liked. They were more expensive than I thought golf equipment would be, but with my new salary, they were still within budget. It was going to be very easy to shop for Graham when his birthday rolled around. Our online shopping was interrupted by the ring of the doorbell. The pizza arrived just as my stomach contemplated eating itself.

"Can we always have dinner together?" I smiled as Graham and I took a seat at the dinner table with the large pizza between us. "It's way more fun eating with you than alone."

"For as long as you'd like," he replied, without hesitation.

I liked that he saw a future with me, but the thought of being hurt again scared me. "What if something bad happens between us?" I mumbled quietly.

Graham paused for a second. "I'm the Graham cracker to your s'mores, remember?" He winked as he passed me a slice of pizza.

I blushed. "And I'm the chocolate to yours."

"Now all we need is a marshmallow." He passionately grabbed my face for a kiss.

From that day on, s'mores were my favorite treat.

19
Daredevil

It was the last full day Graham was in Vegas before he had to take the red-eye flight back to Michigan the following night. We had bonded so much during his trip that I was getting a little sad watching him pack up his stuff. I didn't know how our relationship would grow with him halfway across the country, but I wasn't ready to face that reality. The last couple of days had been the happiest I'd had since I moved to Vegas, and it was all because he'd behaved so lovingly toward me. It was very refreshing to be with a guy who consistently showed me kindness and respect. He was the same person I had always known, and I wondered what would've happened if we got to spend a few more days together.

In honor of Graham's last full day and in celebration of my promotion, Hannah insisted that we wear our matching red bikinis to the pool. She and Graham were the only ones who considered it a good idea. Paige and I were hesitant, knowing that Kyle worked the deck on Sundays. The last time I'd seen him, he was trying to take off my dress after I had just bought him dinner. All the memories of the hurt he caused me started flooding my brain, and I became really apprehensive about seeing him.

"We don't have to go if you don't want to," Graham offered, noticing the change in my demeanor, "but I'll be right by your side the entire time if you decide to go."

Hannah and Paige shared puzzled reactions. They obviously weren't aware of our developing relationship, and Graham's sudden act of compassion toward me was not part of his normal behavior.

"You don't have to treat me like a child, Graham. I'll be fine," I quickly replied, in an effort to try to ease any suspicions.

"Then let's get dressed!" Paige shouted. I knew she was trying to be a good friend and support me in my hesitations, but I could tell she really wanted to spend the day at the pool.

Paige and Hannah quickly forgot about Graham's comment, but Graham's face told a different story. He didn't seem thrilled with my attempt to erase their skepticism around his sudden care for me.

"Next time you could try being a little less harsh," he scoffed as I walked past him toward Paige's room.

It wasn't like me to hide things from my best friend, but who knew what would happen between Graham and me after he went back home. I didn't want to alarm Paige with news about a relationship that might grow as distant as the miles that separated us.

Graham was grabbing a snack from the refrigerator, but paused at the sight of the three of us emerging from Paige's room, looking as hot as the first time we wore the red suits. He had taken the liberty of putting on his swim trunks in the living room while we were getting ready, and we were all equally surprised that they were the same shade of red as our suits.

"You don't have to copy everything I do," I bantered as I filled my bottle with water. "It's actually pretty embarrassing."

"What's embarrassing is you still using your high school water bottle," Graham sarcastically fired back.

I didn't want to admit to anyone that I brought it because Kyle's obligation to check outside drinks gave me an excuse to interact with him. It was a pathetic attempt to gain his attention, but I don't think I had it in me to go to the pool without at least talking to him. The last time we'd hung out was a disaster, and I hadn't heard from him since. He was probably too scared to reach out. We'd had some really good times together, and I didn't think either of us were ready to let that go . . . or maybe I just wasn't ready to let him go.

"Don't forget the key," Paige reminded me in her usual routine before we left the apartment.

Graham was stunned. "Hold on, so you can remember to remind someone about a key, but you can't remember to grab one yourself?"

"At least I know how to put my swimsuit on correctly." She snickered as she pointed out Graham's trunks, which were on backwards.

The girls laughed, and he stammered a bit before turning around and changing his shorts right in front of us. His bare bottom looked extra pale beneath the red shorts.

"What are you doing?" Paige shouted, horrified.

"You clearly were begging to see my butt," he fired back as he finished adjusting his trunks. Paige and Hannah were covering their eyes in terror.

"This is why you're single," Paige croaked under her breath.

Graham sneakily winked at me as we all left the apartment. I made a note to myself to stay out of the sibling banter if he and I ever started dating. It would be impossible to pick either side of the argument. I locked the door behind us as we made our way in the direction of Kyle Kingsley.

We hadn't been to the pool deck in a while, but not much had changed. The same blistering sun was burning against our skin, half-priced appetizers were still being served on Sundays, and Kyle was still standing by the gate flirting with the newest residents. My heart dropped at the sight of him, but my presence didn't seem to affect him much. We made eye contact as our group approached for his usual search of our belongings, but he didn't act like someone who had tried to rip my clothes off the week prior. Nobody said a word while he checked my water bottle, so I decided to end the silence so that he didn't think I had told anyone about what happened between us.

"Good to see you, Kyle," I spoke up. "It's been a while."

Paige was not amused at my attempt to make conversation. I had expressed to her numerous times that I was done with him, but I don't think she fully believed me.

"Good to see you too, Avery," Kyle responded as he handed me back my water. He still hadn't taken the time to screw the cap back on, but I wasn't as annoyed about it as I had been the first time. I was just happy that we were speaking again.

"Let me help you." Graham took the water from me.

I had my bag in one hand and the East Tawas bottle in the other, so I wasn't in the greatest position to twist the lid back on. He had noticed my predicament, and I was hoping Graham's act of kindness would at least pique Kyle's interest, but he let us into the pool area without even a hint of jealousy.

"He didn't seem as bad as you described," Graham said to his sister as we claimed some empty pool chairs.

"You don't even know what he's capable of," Paige insisted. "He looks innocent on the outside but is a terrible human being on the inside."

I rolled my eyes at her, but chose to focus on my latest romance novel instead.

The rest of the day was uneventful. Paige and Hannah tanned in the relentless sun until they retreated to the pool once they couldn't take the heat anymore. Since Graham and I couldn't show our affection in public, he chose to hang around the bar and take advantage of the discounted appetizers. I decided to fill the uninterrupted time by reading my book, but constantly glanced in Kyle's direction. The hurt feelings I'd been remembering earlier were now being replaced with all the good memories we'd had. Technically, we'd never officially ended our pact, so after a few seconds of convincing myself that I was breaking the agreement by not hanging out with him, I put my book down and walked over to the gate.

"So are you going to talk to me or are you going to continue to ignore me?" I asked sarcastically, in an effort to lighten the mood. I think we were both ready to move on from the past, so I didn't want to bring up what had happened the last time we hung out.

Kyle flashed his usual smile at me, which put my anxiety at ease. "I didn't want to get between you and your new boyfriend." He nodded in the direction of Graham, who was sitting at the bar surrounded by every appetizer on the menu.

"He's not my boyfriend," I protested. "He's my best friend's brother."

I was downplaying my relationship with Graham, but we weren't actually dating, so I hadn't exactly lied. Kyle was still staring in his direction, seemingly unconvinced, so I attempted to further erase his concerns.

"He leaves tomorrow," I revealed. "Maybe we could hang out when he's gone?"

It felt desperate, basically begging Kyle to spend time with me, but it was innocent. I still wasn't willing to succumb to his lustful desires, but I at least wanted to get back on good terms with him. I was really having a good time with Graham, but the emotional attachment I had to Kyle wasn't something that would just disappear. He'd come into my life when I was at my lowest. Honestly, I didn't think I'd ever catch the attention of someone as hot as him. There was something thrilling about being with a guy like Kyle. Graham was nice, reliable, and safe. Those were all great qualities, but Kyle was unpredictable and exciting. It was definitely a toxic combination, but my heart couldn't break the trauma bonds it had already formed with him.

"I don't know, Avery," Kyle began. "I feel like we're just looking for different things."

I was becoming increasingly frustrated at his rejection. He used to jump at the idea of spending time with me, so him turning down an invitation to hang out made me feel like every other resident who'd tried to throw themselves at him.

"Hey, Avery!" I heard Graham call out from behind me. "We are heading back to the apartment."

He was accompanied by Paige and Hannah. Paige was clearly infuriated seeing me around Kyle, but Graham didn't seem to mind.

"Yeah, I'll be right there," I said.

I redirected my attention toward Kyle. "Fresh start?" I offered as I stretched out my hand. I wasn't sure why I was the one extending the peace offering when he was the one who'd hurt me, but if I didn't clear the slate, then the rest of the summer would be awkward.

He reached out and shook my hand. "Text me when he's gone."

This was the second deal I had made with the devil. I was hoping this time it wouldn't bite me in the butt, but it was no secret that things between Kyle and me usually ended in disaster. However, for some reason, it was like I was addicted to the thrill. I definitely didn't want to label what I had with Graham as boring, but he was easily the safer option. There was no chase with him. He was emotionally available and ready for commitment. Graham was for sure everything I needed, but Kyle's erratic behavior was everything I gravitated towards. I was just so used to guys treating me poorly that I'd gotten accustomed to the toxicity. I wanted to escape this pattern, but it was easier said than done.

I returned to the group, relieved that I had accomplished what I came to the pool to do. Paige refused to look me in the eye, which made me feel ashamed of my actions. I was still interested in Graham, but I didn't want to continue being on bad terms with Kyle.

"If you even think about messing with that pathetic excuse of a man again," Paige whispered as she pulled me aside, "you're going to have to find a new roommate."

I quickly disregarded her threat because I knew I would choose Graham in the end anyway. He would treat me a lot better than Kyle ever would. There was no competition. Graham Jensen actually wanted to pursue a serious relationship, while Kyle just wanted to play games. I clearly knew which decision would lead to a better future, but somehow I just couldn't fully shake the hold that Kyle Kingsley had on me.

"Truth or dare?" Hannah fired in Paige's direction.

"Definitely dare," Paige returned.

Hannah, Paige, Graham, and I were gathered around the kitchen table after finishing another meal that Graham had paid for. I'd tried to at least cover one dinner while he was here, but he was serious about me not touching my wallet around him.

Sunday nights at our apartment usually ended with watching romantic movies, but with Graham here, everyone thought it was best to play a game.

"I dare you to drink the pickle juice straight out of the jar," Hannah said.

"Those are my good pickles!" I roared as Paige made her way over to the refrigerator.

As many times as I had played the game, I'd never witnessed Paige refuse a dare. Although I was sure drinking pickle juice wouldn't be the highlight of Paige's night, Hannah's dare was light work compared to what I had seen Paige do in the past. One summer in high school, she invited a bunch of friends to spend the night at the Jensens' family lake house. The night had been pretty relaxed until someone decided to dare Paige to jump into the lake naked. She easily accepted the challenge, but hadn't been prepared for the bacteria that entered her system when she accidentally swallowed some of the water as she jumped in. She threw up the entire contents of her stomach the following morning and spent the rest of the weekend in the hospital. The whole ordeal was traumatic, but I was sure she would do it again in a heartbeat. At least the pickle juice that she was gulping now wouldn't send her to the emergency room.

"Delicious," she exclaimed, sitting back down at the table. "Truth or dare, Avery?"

I usually picked truth. It was the safe option, especially since I wasn't as courageous as Paige; however, there was a lot going on in my life that I was hiding, so I decided against it. "Dare," I answered with false confidence.

Paige was shocked. From the hesitation in her response, I could tell she wasn't prepared to pick a dare for me.

"I dare you . . ." she began after carefully considering what my fate would be. "I dare you to dance on the table to the first song that plays from Graham's phone."

Graham hadn't been prepared to be included in my dare but eagerly pulled out his phone and selected a random song from his playlist. I think he was as interested as everyone else around the table to see me make a fool of myself.

To no one's surprise, a country song started wailing from the speakers. I wasn't sure what I'd been expecting him to choose, but definitely not one that had been playing at the music festival where I'd ruined his and Sarah's relationship. Thankfully, I had taken a few line dancing classes back in my younger days, so I wasn't totally horrified at his choice.

I ran into my room and grabbed the cowgirl hat that Graham had bought me for my birthday, then mounted the kitchen table. I performed a few steps from the dances I had learned, which was met with applause and hollers from Paige and Hannah. I think Graham was too stunned to react, but eventually he started clapping to the music. About halfway through the song, I considered my dare complete and returned to my seat. Paige was happy to see me let loose for once, and I was proud of myself for getting outside of my comfort zone, though I still preferred to choose truth.

"Truth or dare," I breathlessly asked Graham.

I felt a lot of power being able to decide his next move. I wanted to allow him a chance to embarrass himself like I just had. He deserved whatever I was going to give him after all the times he had tortured me.

"Truth," he said with a smirk.

Graham relaxed in his chair and shot me a mischievous grin. He'd thrown me off by choosing truth, and he knew it. He always chose dare. He was a daredevil like his sister, and barely kept any secrets. He was an open book, so in the rare case when he did choose truth, there wasn't much that people didn't already know about him.

"Who was the last person you kissed?" I returned boldly.

Graham choked on his water, clearly thrown off by my question. He stared blankly at me, but I returned the pretentious smirk that he'd been giving me earlier. If he wanted to test me, then I was ready. He'd figured not choosing dare would be a way to knock me off my game, but I'd succeeded in making him very uncomfortable.

Paige and Hannah weren't amused by my question, as they assumed nobody at the table would even know the last girl Graham had kissed. I figured he would either accept defeat and lose the game or make up some random person's name, because there was no way he was going to admit the truth.

"Well, are you going to answer or not?" Paige complained after a few moments of silence.

Graham was stalling, and she was losing her patience. A few more seconds passed before he finally collected his thoughts. I figured he'd opted for choosing a fake name, since it had taken him so long to finally respond.

"I can't remember," Graham told the table.

"You're so full of it," Paige muttered, rolling her eyes.

Graham dropped his face and refused to look at me. I wasn't sure if it was because he was ashamed to have denied our kiss or if he was simply accepting defeat. It was his turn in the game, which Paige wasted no time reminding him of, but he didn't seem in the mood to play anymore. Graham loved to mess with me, but he usually didn't shut down like this when I gave him a taste of his own medicine. I almost felt bad for putting him on the spot until he eventually lifted his head, a clever look flashing on his face.

"Truth or dare, Avery," he slyly asked.

"Dare," I answered, unmoved.

"I dare you to go on a date with me tomorrow night before my flight."

This was followed by loud thuds. I wasn't sure if it was my heart beating or Paige's and Hannah's jaws hitting the table. He had avoided my question regarding his kissing history, so I'd assumed he wasn't ready to reveal the feelings we had for each other, but I was clearly mistaken. This time, it was my turn to stare at him speechlessly. I obviously wanted to further explore our relationship, but I'd wanted to at least give Paige a heads-up first. Thanks to Graham, it was a little too late for that. He continued to arrogantly smirk at me as he watched me squirm in my seat, but I wasn't ready to back down yet.

"Only if you let me pay," I responded proudly, in a last-ditch effort to gain the upper hand.

Graham was unable to formulate an answer. I had taken all the shots he had given me and returned even more clever comebacks. He'd been able to tease me all these years, but now he had finally met his match.

"You win, Avery," Graham said, defeated. "You win."

20
Love at First Bite

There was a bouquet of flowers waiting for me on the counter when I walked into the kitchen for my lunch break. I'd never seen such a vibrant shade of red before, but the three dozen roses that Graham had gifted me were so beautiful. The card that accompanied the display congratulated me on my first day as the director of marketing for Ace Modeling Agency, and contained details for a fancy dinner reservation. It was a romantic gesture, but it was also a reminder that Graham was leaving tonight and we wouldn't be able to go on more dates anytime soon. The flowers were going to spend more time in my apartment than he was.

"He calls himself your 'Graham cracker'?" Paige read in disgust as she snatched the card out of my hand. "I think I'm going to be sick."

I ignored her dramatic dry heaves and turned to microwave a bag of popcorn. My usual lunch consisted of a peanut-butter-and-jelly sandwich, but I had run out of bread. It was probably time to start learning how to cook. I could only live off sandwiches, cereal, and microwaved meals for so much longer.

"Where is Graham anyways?" I asked Paige over the popping kernels.

"Golfing," she said. "Don't worry, your Graham cracker said he would be back before your date."

She continued to make gagging sounds that echoed throughout the kitchen. I wasn't sure how long it was going to take her to get used to the fact that I was going on a date with her brother, but at least it wasn't with Kyle.

The microwave beeped, signaling that my lunch was ready to be eaten. I grabbed the steaming bag, which released a delicious buttery aroma into the air. This must've been why Paige was continuing to lurk around the kitchen. Even concerns about her best friend dating her brother could be solved with some fresh popcorn.

"So, why Graham?" she mumbled through a mouthful of my lunch. "He's not that special."

Of course Paige didn't see what I saw in her brother, but she was a sucker for the latest gossip. I wasn't sure how much detail she actually wanted me to provide, considering Graham and I had shared a make-out session in the exact spot where she was standing. I typically loved filling her in on my current romantic interests, but explaining how I fell for her brother didn't seem like the most appropriate topic to discuss.

"I don't know," I answered casually, holding back the details for Paige's sake—and mine too. "We just click."

She didn't ask for any further explanation, just continued to raid the bag of popcorn. I was glad Graham had agreed to allow me to cover the bill tonight since he'd paid for everything else during his trip, but I was even more grateful considering I would be ordering the entire menu. The bag of popcorn was my only source of food until then, and I was definitely planning on ordering at least two appetizers.

Paige's question really got my mind spinning though. Why was I so attracted to Graham? He was obviously very easy on the eyes, with his gorgeous face and muscular body, but there was way more to him. He had seen me grow up, which made him able to read my emotions and understand my feelings on a level that no other guy had before. He possessed the kindest heart and the sweetest soul of any human being on the planet. Graham was everything that Kyle wasn't. He treated me the way I deserved to be treated, and he never left me questioning him or myself. I was finally going to put a stop to my endless cycle of choosing men who were not right for me. Graham was the one. It had just taken me a while to finally realize what I needed.

When I eventually snapped myself back to reality after being lost in my thoughts, I realized I hadn't eaten any of my lunch yet, and my break was over in ten minutes. I reached my hand into the bag of popcorn, but was met with a mixture of hot air and unpopped kernels.

"You should make two bags next time," Paige said as she licked the butter off the ends of her fingers. She retreated back into her room, the temptation of food no longer keeping her in the kitchen. "Maybe your Graham cracker will bring you a snack." With a wink, she shut the door.

I was frustrated that she hadn't saved me any popcorn, but I was mostly just emotional that today was Graham's last day in Vegas. If it hadn't been my first day under my new title, I probably would have taken it off to spend it with him. He was the Graham cracker to my s'mores, and I was the chocolate to his.

"Now all I need is a marshmallow," I said to myself, staring at the bouquet of roses on the counter.

"Ladies first," Graham insisted as he opened the door to the restaurant.

He'd chosen a nice steakhouse on a hill that provided a beautiful view of the entire city. It was obvious he wasn't expecting anyone other than himself to cover the bill, but I wasn't going to let him change my mind. He deserved the fancy dinner over dim candlelight surrounded by city views as much as anyone could have. I figured I would let him think he was paying until the actual check came, just in case he tried to order something light.

"This place is amazing," I commented as we glanced over the menu. Going to new restaurants always gave me anxiety, so although I appeared to be looking over my choices with great intent, I had already spent an hour narrowing down my options before we arrived.

"Order whatever you want." Graham smiled through his perfect teeth. "But may I suggest the filet mignon?"

His comment made it official—he had no intention of letting me touch my wallet tonight. The filet was one of the most exquisite and expensive items on the menu. Graham's conscience would never allow him to let his date cover that. I reached into my purse to confirm my wallet was still there just in case he tried to sneak it out of my possession when I wasn't looking. Fortunately, it was, but I was becoming very concerned about how I was going to manage paying for the dinner. It became clear that I would have to find a way to go behind his back, because he was in no place to be convinced otherwise.

"Can I get the lovely couple anything to drink besides water?" the waiter asked as he approached our table.

Graham nodded in my direction, indicating that I was to answer first.

"I'm good with water, but we will have one of every appetizer," I politely responded.

Graham's eyes widened slightly at my request. He tried to hide his reaction, but I knew him well enough to know when something caught him off guard. His astonished expression turned into a playful grin when he realized what game we were playing. We were both going to insist on paying and were trying to do anything in our power to be the one to lay their credit card down at the end of the night. He'd started off strong by intimidating me with his selection of the restaurant, but I figured my outrageous order was a better move.

"Whatever the lady wants," Graham affirmed when the waiter turned to him to confirm that my order was indeed sincere. "She had a light lunch."

Graham winked in my direction. The purpose of ordering all the extra food was to coerce him into letting me cover the bill, but my grumbling stomach would also benefit from my power move. I had explained to him my frustrations with his sister's eating behaviors on the car ride over here, but he'd only focused on the part of the story where I couldn't eat anything else because I didn't know how to work anything other than a microwave. After making fun of me, he offered to give me cooking lessons. The few kernels that had made it into my stomach had not been able to tame the beast of my hunger, but with Graham's help, I was hoping my days of eating microwaved foods would soon be over.

I knew ten appetizers was excessive when I placed the order, but I wasn't prepared for all the attention that it drew to our table. Extra wait staff had to be utilized in order to bring out all of the dishes, and it caused quite the scene. The rest of the restaurant probably thought we were insanely rich or insanely crazy.

"I think I went a little overboard," I admitted as I evaluated all of the food.

"Maybe just a little," Graham agreed, chuckling.

We dug into our appetizers, and as much as I was embarrassed by my order, I had no regrets. Each bite was an explosion of delicious flavor. There wasn't a single dish that I didn't like. I happily danced in my chair as I continued to flood my taste buds with amazing food.

"I'm going to marry the chef," I cried out as I finished another plate.

Graham was as delighted by the food as I was, but I don't think he was inclined to wed the one who'd prepared it.

"He's one lucky guy," Graham noted as he took a few more bites.

A few minutes later, the waiter returned to clear out the empty plates and take our order for the main course. The appetizers were nearly finished, and I didn't think my stomach could handle more food. Graham noticed my lethargic state and notified the waiter that we were going to pass on any additional platters.

"Maybe we can try the filet next time," I suggested. Graham was much larger than me, so I wasn't sure whether his stomach had reached its limits like mine had.

"What about dessert?" the waiter inquired.

My eyes suddenly lit up, and my stomach magically found just enough room to squeeze in a few more calories.

"One of everything?" Graham joked, noticing my eagerness.

"How about just the ice cream?" I laughed.

The waiter gathered our dessert menus and returned to the kitchen. I'd really wanted to try the steak that Graham had suggested earlier, but it would give us a reason to come back.

"So what do you want, Avery?" Graham blurted out.

"Ice cream," I informed him. "We just ordered it." I wasn't sure if he was having a lapse in memory or hinting at ordering another dessert.

"I meant with me," he clarified. "I'm going back to Michigan tonight, and I don't want to leave without knowing what you want from this."

Our relationship had obviously grown over the time that he'd been here. I wasn't ready for us to go our separate ways, but I wasn't sure I was able to trust a man again, especially with thousands of miles between us. The fear of being hurt again heavily weighed on me, but deep down, I knew Graham was worth the risk.

"I guess I'm willing to see where this goes," I reluctantly admitted.

He smiled back at me. We were too perfect of a match to let our budding relationship fade without at least giving it a chance. I really wanted our tight bond to develop into a committed relationship, but I didn't want to get my hopes up yet. I continued to imagine what life would be like if I started officially dating Graham as he excused himself to use the restroom. However, my fantasy was quickly interrupted by the waiter bringing out a decadent scoop of vanilla ice cream.

"Excuse me, sir," I said as I frantically pulled out my credit card before Graham returned. "Can I cover the bill now?"

The waiter gave me a funny look and laughed. "I'm sorry, young lady, I am not bringing out the check."

"Why not?" I stammered.

I knew gender roles had been a major force in society back in the day, but this was modern times, and I didn't need the waiter withholding the bill so that the man could pay.

"I'm not making the head chef pay for his meal," he told me.

"Head chef?" I cried out.

"His home base is our location in the wonderful state of Michigan, but he occasionally stops by to help out around here," the man informed me. "If I'm not mistaken, he played a round of golf with our executive team today."

"And I beat every single one of them," Graham interjected as he returned to the table.

My mouth hung open in complete shock.

"What?" He dug into the ice cream. "Did you think my parents were the ones who taught me how to cook eggs and bacon like that?"

Graham continued to eat the dessert as he basked in the glory of watching me process my recent discovery. I knew he had pursued his dream of being a chef, but I hadn't known he sometimes cooked at the very restaurant he'd taken me to.

"You win, Graham Jensen," I admitted. "You win."

21
Battle Cry

Paige drove through the darkness of the desert night back to our apartment. I stared out the window, swallowing back the lump of tears that was stuck in my throat. The radio was on low enough that Paige would've noticed even a sniffle out of me, so I was extra cautious about the noises I was making. It was hard to say goodbye to Graham, but at least Paige had given us a moment of privacy before she and I left. He'd promised me he would be back soon, but the taste of his lips was already fading, like my hope of finding happiness again without him here.

I watched the cars drive past us in the opposite direction, wondering if anyone else was headed to the airport to watch the man of their dreams fly away. Surely I couldn't be the only one falling for someone who lived halfway across the country. There was probably an abundance of support groups for people in situations similar to mine. However, even in a roomful of people, I still probably would've felt alone.

"Are you hungry?" Paige began as she turned into the nearest drive-through.

"Starving," I confessed.

The only feeling battling my profound sadness was hunger. It had only been about two hours since I had inhaled an entire menu's worth of appetizers and a scoop of ice cream, but apparently the anxiety of watching Graham disappear behind the airport doors burned all those calories away.

Las Vegas was one of those cities where everything was open throughout all hours of the night. Back in Michigan, most establishments had their lights off by ten, and anyone who had the late-night munchies was limited to the snacks in their home or at the local gas station. In Vegas, the competition was so fierce that businesses couldn't even afford to close. This made it very convenient for Paige to find a place for me to scarf down another meal, even if it was almost eleven o'clock at night.

"Can I get two cheeseburgers, two medium sodas, and two large fries?" Paige asked the speaker that was taking her order. She continued to browse the menu before turning her attention toward me. "Do you want anything else?"

"A filet mignon," I muttered under my breath.

She stared at me inquisitively. "I don't think they serve that here," she remarked as she pulled up to the second window.

We ate our burgers in the solitude of the fast-food parking lot. Paige wasn't the best multitasker, and she definitely wasn't going to let her fries get cold, so we sat in her car while we stuffed our faces. It was hard to go from eating at a five-star steakhouse to a subpar burger chain, but this was going to be my new normal until I learned how to cook or until Graham returned to cook for me. I stared hesitantly at the soggy fries, which radiated scents of salt and oil, but I was too hungry to resist. The burger bun was the same consistency as the fries, which made it crumble apart under the force of my fingers. A mixture of cheese and ketchup ran down my arm after each bite.

My phone vibrated in my lap, but my fingers were too messy to pick it up. I glanced down at the screen and noticed the incoming text from Graham. I quickly wiped my greasy hands against the sides of my legs, since my only alternative was the wrapper that the burger was encased in. Perhaps Nevada burger chains sold their napkins separately.

Miss you already.

I smiled at the phone. He felt like home, and I hadn't been prepared for the empty space in my heart when he left. Paige noticed my obnoxious grin, but refrained from asking any questions. I was sure she could guess who the message was from and didn't want to ruin her appetite over the thought of her brother spilling his emotions to her best friend.

I wanted nothing more than for Graham to ditch his flight and be waiting at our apartment when we got back. There was a giant void when he wasn't around. He knew how to make me feel seen, and without him, I felt empty inside. Before diving back into my burger, I grabbed my phone and started crafting a message. It didn't take long for me to formulate what I was going to say. It was short, but I had been thinking about it for a while.

I typed two quick words and reread them, just to make sure it was what I wanted to say.

He left.

I quickly hit send, picked my burger back up, and patiently waited for Kyle Kingsley to respond.

The drive over to Kyle's house was filled with agonizing thoughts that turned my tormented mind into a shameful cocoon. My head was filled with the sound of what Paige would have said if she had seen me leave the apartment. I was ashamed knowing what Graham would've thought if he knew where I was going, but I was only trying to fill the space in my heart that he'd left.

Kyle was the only person I knew who could temporarily solve my loneliness. I knew my emotional connection to him was not the healthiest, but he was the first guy who had made me feel seen after my breakup with Ethan. When Kyle looked at me, I saw a fiery desire in his eyes. I'd never been a huge fan of my own body, but to Kyle, it was the holy grail. Graham made me feel pretty, but Kyle made me feel sexy. I craved the attention that Kyle gave me when he desperately wanted me. It was exhilarating knowing that Kyle admired my appearance, but deep down inside, I knew trouble was on the horizon.

After I had texted Kyle, he agreed to let me come over if I brought him some food, so I made a quick stop at the pizza parlor next to Exe Apartments before heading over. Luckily for me, it was a weekday, so the pizza promotion applied. I wasn't thrilled by the idea of buying another one of Kyle's meals, especially since he had never returned the favor, but I was desperate to see him again.

Since I had already been to his apartment, it was easier to navigate the maze of pathways that ran throughout the complex this time. There was still an anonymity to the units that made them hard to tell apart, but I recognized his deteriorating door, which stared back at me when I knocked on it. The seconds it took Kyle to answer felt like hours. Graham and I weren't officially together, so technically showing up here in the middle of the night wasn't necessarily cheating, but the knot in my stomach begged to differ. A wave of gut-wrenching guilt crashed over me, and I felt like that was my signal to turn around, but before I could fully process my actions, I was already inside.

"I'm assuming you don't want any of this pizza since you only got a medium this time," Kyle observed as he took the box from my hands.

"I'm okay," I answered. "I already ate."

I wasn't exactly planning on eating again since I had just finished a burger and fries not too long ago, but I hadn't been expecting Kyle's first words to me to be an ungracious comment about the amount of food I'd brought over.

"You look good today," he said as we made our way over to the kitchen table.

"Thanks. So do you," I replied, watching his mouth water over the sizzling cheese and garlic crust.

Kyle's apartment looked exactly how I remembered it from the first time I came over. However, without Eli, Mike, and their girlfriends, the place felt more abandoned. I continued to mentally criticize Kyle's space as he devoured his dinner. It had only been roughly five minutes since I had arrived, and a third of the pizza was already gone. He was eating as if it were his first meal of the day, and I was wondering if this was how I'd looked when I ate those eggs and bacon in front of Graham.

"What a mighty fine meal, wouldn't you say?" I said in a tone similar to the one I'd used with Graham.

Kyle paused for a minute but continued to chew his food. "Why are you talking like that?" he managed to ask in between bites of pizza.

I hadn't been expecting Kyle to pick up on the joke as quickly as Graham had, but I was hoping he'd offer at least some playful banter. It felt wrong to ruminate over a memory I shared with Graham and then try to recreate it with Kyle, but it was awkward just watching him eat. I tried not to compare the two men, but I couldn't find any of the characteristics that Graham had in Kyle. It made me realize that the fact that they both gave me similar feelings did not mean they were similar people.

"So what did you do today?" I asked Kyle, again attempting to break the silence.

"Chilled," he answered, fully focused on eating.

He was becoming increasingly annoyed that I was interrupting his dinner with questions, but the least he could do was engage in conversation, since I was the one who'd paid for the pizza. In his defense, he was usually more talkative and willing to joke around once his stomach was full, so I spent the rest of his meal on my phone, trying to drown out the sound of him chewing. I watched a few videos of Toby, Leo, Tubs, and Benny that Paige had sent me earlier in the day. As expected, the older cats were peacefully sunbathing while Benny was tearing apart furniture. I was laughing over his cute little attempt to attack the couch pillows when I heard Kyle close the pizza box and add it to an already overflowing pile in the corner.

"You sure eat a lot of pizza," I commented, as the stack couldn't have contained any less than ten boxes. A few flies were swirling around the tower of cardboard, and I didn't even want to know how long they had been there.

"Yeah, I do," Kyle confirmed with a devilish smirk, "and I haven't had to pay for a single one of them." He pressed away from the table and wiped the remaining crumbs onto the floor. "Let's go to my room."

I already felt uneasy being alone with him in his kitchen, so I was hesitant to follow him into his bedroom, but I felt like I had no other choice. I was afraid he would kick me out if I refused to cooperate.

"Um, sure," I replied as I warily left my chair and followed him.

Kyle's bedroom was cleaner than the rest of his apartment, which wasn't saying much. It also wasn't that hard to keep a room clean that only consisted of a bean bag chair and a mattress that laid directly on the floor. There were a few articles of clothing piled up in the corners, but no additional furniture.

Kyle shut the door behind us and took a seat on the bed, which forced me to join him—otherwise he would've been eye-level with my knees. I considered getting comfortable in the bean bag chair instead, but I wasn't sure what creatures were living inside its cracks and crevices.

I was going behind my best friend's back and risking my relationship with Graham for this beloved alone time with Kyle, but the dim lighting, musty odor, and uncomfortable mattress were making it hard to enjoy the moment. As much as I typically tried to find ways to hang out with Kyle, all I could think about was how I couldn't wait to get back home and call Graham. The fiery desire and lustful attraction that I used to have for Kyle were gradually fading with each minute that passed.

I regretted coming over and wanted to leave. There was a tiny beam of light from the kitchen that shone in under Kyle's door, illuminating my exit route. The rest of the space was filled with complete darkness. In the light, I was blinded by Kyle's flawless body and charismatic demeanor, but in the dark, all I found myself doing was searching for a way to escape him.

"You're so beautiful," he said in the abyss of darkness.

I was flattered, but unless he possessed some type of night vision, he was either lying or simply picturing how I'd looked earlier, considering no human would've possibly been able to see me. His strange ability to be unaffected by the pitch-black made my nerves start to intensify, and I was growing more uncomfortable. I wasn't sure if he could detect my concern, but as I was plotting to leave, he grabbed my face and shoved his tongue down my throat before I even had time to react.

"Kyle, stop!" I tried to shout, but my voice was muffled by his mouth being locked onto mine.

I attempted to push him off me, but my strength was no match against his. He proceeded to fight his way on top of me while pulling at my clothes. The more I pushed him away, the harder he held on. I couldn't escape his grip and figured the best way to get out of the situation was to pretend to enjoy it. Maybe he would let his guard down if I stopped struggling. I abruptly ceased any attempt at escaping his arms and proceeded to let him remove my top. His hands explored where they pleased, and I even kissed him back a bit to make my performance more convincing. My lack of resistance excited him, and he continued to push for more.

"Take off your clothes," I demanded from under him.

Kyle paused, clearly startled by my sudden request. "Eager girl," he noted, pleased, as he lifted himself off me to remove his shirt. "This is the type of Avery I've been waiting for."

Once I felt his weight shift off me, I took my leg and, with one quick motion, forced it straight into his stomach. He fell to the center of the mattress in a fury of pain, moaning in agony. While he tended to the blunt force trauma that I'd inflicted on his midsection, I quickly got up and ran for the light. I flung the door open and stepped out as my eyes readjusted. My keys and purse were still on the kitchen table, and I lunged for them before sprinting out of the apartment. I slammed the door behind me and raced back through the maze of corridors. Over my loud breathing, I could hear Kyle's front door open as I was maneuvering my way out of the complex.

"You're getting closer and closer!" Kyle shouted after me. "Maybe next time you'll finally give in."

This was all a game to him. He thought it was funny to see how far he could push my limits before I eventually stopped him. My boundaries were just a joke to him.

I continued to weave my way around the neighborhood until I finally reached the parking lot. Once I'd locked myself in the safety of my car, I retrieved my phone from my purse. I debated calling Paige, but resorted to texting Graham instead.

Miss you too. Please come back soon.

I hit send and quickly drove home. Kyle Kingsley was no Graham Jensen.

22
Terrible Twos

I wasn't a stranger to holding Paige's hair back while she puked her guts out. We'd lived together in college. Therefore, I had firsthand experience watching the effects of the drinks men would buy her at bars. After each night she spent hovering over a toilet, she swore that she would never get that drunk again. It always turned out to be an empty promise, since she would end up in the same situation the following weekend. It was hard for her to resist the free alcohol and free attention. However, this time, an undercooked burger was the source of her sickness.

I took the day off work to care for her while she spent the entire morning emptying her stomach. Needless to say, it wasn't the prettiest of sights. Fortunately, it was a lot easier to request time off as a director than a new hire. I didn't have heartless middle managers trying to prohibit my ability to utilize my vacation time.

"I'm never eating a burger again," Paige vowed.

We spent a few more hours in the bathroom while her body rid itself of the bad meat. I was eventually able to walk her to her bed once we were confident that she was done puking. She looked paler than normal, but I was hoping we had made it through the worst part. I turned on her TV and chose one of her favorite movies. We watched a few scenes, but then she started to get restless.

"Can you do me a favor?" Paige faintly croaked. "Can you microwave me a bag of popcorn?"

It was a good sign that she was requesting food, so I happily made my way to the kitchen. I remembered how annoyed I'd been the last time she ate my entire bag of popcorn, but this time, I was excited to make it for her. Once the microwave finished converting the tiny kernels into a buttery snack, I poured the contents into a bowl so that she wouldn't get her hands dirty. However, I saved the bag for her, because I knew she liked to lick the butter off the sides of it.

"Wow, Avery, you're almost as good a chef as Graham," Paige complimented when I handed her the freshly made popcorn. Apparently, her sense of humor had returned with her appetite. "Can you do me one more favor?" she begged.

"Anything for you."

She grabbed my hand. I knew it was going to be something more serious than fetching her some more food from the way she was grazing her thumb back and forth over my knuckles.

"Can you watch the Thompsons for me today?" she cautiously asked.

"Absolutely not!" I exclaimed, without hesitation.

When I'd said I would do anything for Paige, I meant that I would do anything except watch tiny children. I was almost as bad at babysitting as I was at cooking. Paige must've thrown up her common sense along with the rotten burger.

"It's only for a few hours," she pleaded. "Riley is six years old, and she is the funniest little girl. Wyatt is two, and he is the sweetest boy you'll ever meet."

I rolled my eyes as she continued to explain how great the Thompsons were. Little did she know that describing the kids and their ages hurt her argument more than it helped it.

"If you help me out," Paige negotiated, "I promise to stop giving you a hard time about liking Graham."

In all honesty, I would have rather she agreed to never bad-mouth Kyle, but she probably would've thrown up again if I'd proposed that alternative.

"Fine." I shook her hand. "No more comments about me and your brother."

I fetched a few more blankets and made sure Paige was comfortable while she notified the parents that I would be covering for her. They clearly had a lot of faith in her if they were willing to blindly trust her replacement. Paige was an amazing caretaker, and I was hoping that the family wasn't expecting me to be anything like her. My goal was just to return the kids in the same condition that they were handed to me.

"You know, I would've watched the Thompsons without the extra incentive," I told her, opening her curtains and letting the sunlight flood her bedroom. Part of me was concerned that the popcorn was going to make a reappearance, but the color was starting to return to Paige's face, and her energy was slowly coming back.

"And you know I would've agreed to not talk about your feelings for Graham or your inability to cook." Paige laughed.

I grabbed the bowl of popcorn out of her lap, winking as I took a handful, then handed it back to her. "I'll remember that the next time you ask me to make you a snack."

"Don't forget a key," she said enthusiastically as I left her room.

I laughed at the consistency of Paige's reminder, despite the fact that she'd been tied to a toilet not too long ago. No matter the circumstances, she was always going to be the same old Paige. Even a little food poisoning couldn't break her spirit.

The Thompson family had more money than they knew what to do with. Their five-bedroom, six-bathroom mansion sat on two acres of land in a prestigious gated community. I waited until the parents had left before exploring the best parts of the house that had been displayed on the tour they'd given me before departing. At first, I thought Mr. and Mrs. Thompson's efforts to show me around were just a kind gesture, but I quickly realized that it was mostly intended to prevent me from getting lost. I almost requested a copy of the floor plan before they left.

I spent most of the day in the west wing, where the third kitchen, playroom, and children's bedrooms were located. Their six-year-old daughter, Riley, wasted no time showing me her room, which was an explosion of pink, princess-themed decor. Stuffed animals and baby dolls were scattered around her bed, and pageant dresses filled the closet. The space was as outgoing as she was, and every inch revealed another part of her personality.

The two-year-old boy, Wyatt, had been napping when I arrived, so I didn't get a chance to meet him. His parents had handed me a baby monitor, as he was supposed to remain asleep through the duration of my stay. I only had to watch the kids for a few hours, and one was sleeping. Maybe being a nanny wasn't as hard as I'd thought it would be.

Once Riley finished telling me the names of every one of her dolls, she and I made our way to the kitchen with a handful of crayons and a coloring book. The Thompsons were very strict about the amount of time their children spent using electronics and had encouraged me to engage in alternative activities. Riley expressed her love of drawing, so we ended up entertaining ourselves with art. I watched her flip through the pages of the coloring book before finally choosing a nature scene.

"Do you have a boyfriend?" she asked as she decided which blue crayon she was going to use to fill in the sky.

"No, I don't," I said shyly. I wasn't sure why being questioned by a six-year-old was intimidating, but her curious mind left no topic off the table.

"Why don't you have a boyfriend?" Riley continued. Clearly my love life was at the top of her mind.

"The boy that I like lives far away," I replied honestly.

I often pictured what it would be like to be in an interrogation room, most likely because I wanted to be prepared in case I was ever brought in for questioning by the police as a coconspirator to a Paige revenge plan gone wrong, but also because I watched a lot of television. The crime shows I occasionally tuned in for when taking a break from my romantic comedies usually showed the culprit confessing within the first few minutes. I swore to myself that if I was ever in that situation, I would hold out for at least twenty-four hours before detailing all of Paige's wrongdoings. I still believed I would be able to keep my lips sealed for a while, but I wasn't sure how long I would last if a child were the one interrogating me.

"Why don't you like a boy that lives here?" I'd figured coloring would keep Riley's mind busy, but she continued to fire questions in my direction.

"The boy that lives far away is nicer than the boys that live close," I reasoned, even though my argument was solely based on the relationships I had with Kyle and Graham.

"My daddy's nice," Riley quickly countered.

"Your dad is really nice," I responded, hoping she wouldn't tell her parents that the new nanny had said bad things about her dad. "Wyatt is nice too."

From the baby monitor, I could see the toddler peacefully napping in his bed. He seemed like a sweet baby, and I couldn't help but wonder if he would grow up to be a Kyle or a Graham.

"Paige said your pool boy is mean," Riley casually noted.

I immediately knew who she was referring to. It was obvious that Paige wasn't shy about sharing her feelings regarding Kyle, but I had figured she would draw the line at some point. Apparently, even the kids she babysat for weren't off-limits when it came to her avid gossiping.

"He's not mean," I said. "He's just misunderstood."

"What does that mean?" Riley asked. She paused her coloring to hear my answer.

I didn't really know exactly what I meant, but I was in too deep to back out.

"It means he is a good person who sometimes does bad things," I explained.

Riley resumed coloring, so I assumed my response had finally satisfied her inquisitive mind.

"Has he ever done anything bad to you?" she pressed.

Of all the questions Riley had thrown at me, this was the one I was least prepared for. I truly did not know how to respond. Had Kyle actually crossed a line the other night, or was it my own actions that had caused his behavior? I did reach out to him in the middle of the night, and it wasn't like he'd forced me to follow him into his bedroom. He might have been under the impression that he was giving me what I wanted, unaware that he had gone too far. I replayed the events before eventually coming to a conclusion.

"Not on purpose," I insisted, more to myself than to Riley, who had already turned her attention to choosing her next color. "He didn't do anything bad to me on purpose."

23

Risky Appetite

Saturdays had easily become my favorite day of the week. I used to spend them soaking in the envy of watching Paige scramble to her room for her weekly call with her mom, but now they were spent preparing to talk to Graham. Navigating our relationship with thousands of miles between us proved to be tough, but we were intentional about our communication and made time for each other.

We'd decided to reserve Saturday nights for dates, which involved calling each other while we ate dinner. Graham had sent me instructions on how to cook spaghetti earlier in the day and challenged me to prepare it before he called. I was excited to make my first meal in a while that utilized the stove, but it was harder than I remembered. I pictured myself cooking the best pasta I had ever tasted and surprising Paige with the delicious leftovers when she returned from work, but it took me twenty minutes just to figure out how to turn on the burner. A gaseous odor filled the air once I finally ignited it, and I hoped our apartment wasn't going to end up in flames.

Luckily, I was able to successfully boil the water, but when I went to add the salt, a lot more rushed out than I had anticipated. The water and half of Paige's salt had to be poured down the drain. Graham had assured me that spaghetti was an easy dinner to make, but I was already on my second pot of water, and the smell of gas still filled the air.

Opening the jar of tomato sauce also posed an issue. Apparently, these lids had been designed with bodybuilders in mind, considering the average human didn't possess enough strength to open them on their own. I tried banging the side of the jar against the kitchen counter, but was considering just eating the noodles plain after my millionth attempt at opening it. A knock at the door put a pause to my frustrations, and I hoped there was a strong man on the other side coming to rescue me from my pasta crisis.

The door was unlocked, as it always was, but Hannah and Paige knew that and would've been inside ridiculing my cooking skills by now if they'd been the ones knocking. In hindsight, I should've been more careful on what I wished for, because there actually was a muscular man on the other side of the door waiting for me, except he wasn't here to help me cook.

"You left this at my apartment," Kyle explained as he handed me back the shirt that he'd forcibly ripped off me the night I was over.

"Oh, thanks," I mumbled as I took it from him.

He continued to stand in the doorway. He didn't look as though he had anything further to say, but he didn't show any signs of leaving either.

"Do you want to come in?" I offered, fully expecting him to decline.

"Sure," he replied, stepping into my apartment.

I closed the door behind him and returned to tending to my pasta. My date with Graham was in half an hour, but I wasn't expecting Kyle to stay long. Disaster usually struck sooner than that, anyway.

"Aren't you supposed to be working?" I asked as I tried to figure out how to make spaghetti without the sauce.

"Pool closed early for maintenance." Kyle was staring intently at me. He seemed to know that I wasn't comfortable in the kitchen, furrowing his brow at every move I made. "Do you need help with that?" he offered when he saw me wrestling with the tomato jar.

I wanted to show him that I was an independent woman who didn't need a guy's help, but realizing there was no way I was going to be able to open it on my own, I reluctantly handed him the jar. He took it from me, and in a matter of seconds, the lid was removed.

"Thanks," I said, grateful that I wasn't going to be eating just noodles for dinner.

My glorious triumph in finally having an open jar of sauce quickly turned into anguish when I realized I didn't know what the next step was.

"What are you making?" Kyle inquired as he browsed the kitchen.

"I'm trying to make spaghetti," I said, "but it's a lot harder than it looks."

He examined the disaster before him. Water and salt had flooded the countertops. Pots and pans surrounded the stove from my search for the right equipment. There was a mess in every part of the kitchen I had been in, and all I had to show for it was a pot of boiling water that didn't even have salt in it yet.

Kyle swiftly grabbed the uncooked noodles and added them to the pot of boiling water. He carefully stirred in a pinch of salt and adjusted the temperature of the stove. All kitchen equipment must work the same way, because he wasted no time in turning on another burner to low heat and putting a pot with the tomato sauce on it.

"Do you have any garlic bread?" he asked over the steam and bubbling sauce.

I nodded my head and retrieved some from the freezer. He scoffed a little bit, but he knew how to prepare it without even reading the directions on the back. I was in awe of Kyle's abilities. He was a natural cook and easily navigated around the kitchen. The gassy smell that once filled the apartment had now been replaced with the smell of tomato and garlic.

"Where did you learn to cook?" I asked as I watched him tend to the pots on the stove.

"My parents taught me before they passed," he told me.

I felt bad bringing up such a sensitive topic. It was evident Kyle was still grieving over the recent loss of his parents, and I didn't want to make him feel uncomfortable.

"Do you want to learn?" He handed me a spoon.

I hesitantly grabbed it from him and started stirring the water-and-noodle mixture. He grabbed the saltshaker and emptied a few dashes of it into my palm. I slowly added it to the pot and watched it disappear into the steaming water.

"You're already a pro," Kyle complimented.

I beamed with happiness as I continued to stir. Although I wasn't doing much, I felt so accomplished. This was the most cooking I had done in months.

"You take direction so well," he seductively noted as he inched toward me. "Let's see what else you can do." I took a giant gulp as he continued to move closer. "Don't worry," he said. "I'll talk you through it."

Kyle picked me up and lifted me onto the counter. He positioned himself between my legs and wrapped his large hand around my neck. His grip was a lot tighter than I was expecting. My airways were becoming increasingly restricted, but I continued to withstand his strength. His eyes were piercing, almost soulless, as he watched my breaths become shallower. The smile that spread across his face revealed that he was enjoying this a lot more than I was.

His tongue eventually made its way to my neck, rewarding me for all the pain I was enduring. I reveled in the blissful feeling and was disappointed when the sensation ended. Kyle had paused to remove his shirt, and when he reached for mine, I didn't offer any resistance. My heart wasn't ready to succumb to his temptations, but my body was more than willing. I watched him remove my top, wallowing in the sight of my exposed skin. He insistently tugged at the rest of his clothes, and before I knew it, his naked body was staring back at me. He desperately wanted my clothes to accompany his on the floor and he reached for the fly of my pants. I brushed away his hand, still not able to take things to the next level. I could see frustration bubbling within him. He tried again, but this time I batted him away with even more force.

"Kyle, stop," I demanded.

I held firm in my stance against taking this any further, but I didn't know if I could stop him. It seemed as if nothing was going to get in his way this time. He had me exactly where he wanted me. He salivated over me one more time before finally deciding he was ready to see everything. Lunging for me again, he abruptly stopped when the blaring fire alarm began to echo throughout the apartment. The garlic bread was burning to a crisp under the intense heat of the oven. Kyle urgently found the oven mitts and removed the charcoal bread, but the alarm was still roaring.

We both rapidly dressed, not knowing if the fire department was going to show up or if we were going to have to leave the premises. I grabbed a towel and started fanning the smoke alarm. Kyle followed suit, and after a few minutes, it finally ceased. The kitchen was filled with thick smoke and the smell of burning garlic.

"I think it's ready," I announced sarcastically, staring at the blackened bread.

Kyle removed the noodles and sauce from the stovetop while I opened a few windows to welcome in some fresh air. I rummaged through the cabinets until I found the glass plates and fancy silverware. We each served ourselves a hefty portion of pasta, which had turned out better than expected despite being slightly overdone.

"Thanks for helping me cook," I said between bites. "I had no idea what I was doing. Cooking is not my strong suit."

"I know." Kyle nodded. "Remember when you tried to bring me that tuna sandwich for lunch?"

"It was turkey," I corrected.

"Even worse."

We laughed at the memory. I could still picture the cold deli meat disintegrating between my fingers. Regardless, he didn't seem totally disgusted by the idea of turkey. I'd known he wasn't a ham guy.

The heavy smoke eventually cleared out of the kitchen, and we were able to enjoy a normal dinner together. We didn't discuss the events prior to the alarm going off. He probably didn't think he did anything wrong, and I continued to make excuses for his behavior. I thought we were making progress in our friendship, but it was obvious where things stood between us. Kyle only wanted one thing from me, and I wasn't willing to give that to him. We were at the point in our relationship where we both realized neither party was going to get what they wanted. I refused to engage in anything casual with him, while he insisted on not having a serious relationship with me.

We continued to indulge in our pasta as if this were just another ordinary night. If I had pulled out my phone at any time during my dinner with Kyle, I would've noticed the seven missed calls from Graham and four from Paige. It had been over an hour since our scheduled dinner. I had missed my date with Graham, but things could've been worse. At least my apartment didn't burn down.

24
All Good Things Come to an End

I was able to convince Graham and Paige that the food poisoning from the burger I'd initially escaped had finally caught up to me. It was the only excuse I could come up with for why I had missed our date. I miraculously made a full recovery the following morning, but Graham continued to check on me and even offered to fly out.

Three weeks later, he was still insisting on sending me medicine, soup, and my favorite candies. I was secretly hoping his thoughtful gifts would stop, because the guilt that accompanied every package he sent was eating me alive. I eventually felt so bad that I ended up buying him the set of golf clubs he really wanted. Graham almost didn't accept them because he knew how much they cost, but I insisted he deserved them.

The clubs were really expensive, but spoiling Graham was one of the luxuries I allowed myself to indulge in. My paychecks were really beginning to add up, and I was actually starting to accumulate a good amount of money in my savings account. In addition to the gifts for Graham, I also bought Paige a high-tech litter box for her cats and treated myself to a new set of kitchenware. I was taking Graham's cooking advice really seriously and even learned to bake a casserole.

I thought my huge promotion was going to expose my lack of knowledge of the modeling industry, but it turned out my new position was very similar to the role I used to have. My experience handling the complaints on our social media pages had provided me with insight into what our agency was truly lacking. It gave me a hands-on perspective that the other directors at my level didn't have. I spent most of my days explaining everything

I had gathered in my previous role or training others to extract the data.

Despite my short time at the company, I was gaining a lot of respect, and there were already whispers about an additional promotion on the horizon. The time I used to spend stressing over the job I hated were now spent hanging out with Paige and Hannah. Fortunately, they still excluded me from their cat playdates, especially since Benny was still a huge troublemaker and didn't get along well with Tubs, but I occasionally hung out with Toby and Leo when Paige was away.

Paige still spent most of her time at the Thompsons' house, and they even took her on a weekend trip to California. She spoke so highly of her job that Hannah decided to try being a nanny. I assured her that if I could do it, she definitely could too. I actually missed Riley sometimes, but I definitely could've gone without her millions of questions.

I was considering joining Paige for a few hours today so that I could actually meet Wyatt and see Riley again, but it was Labor Day weekend, which meant the pool was closing soon. I'd tried to convince Graham to move his flight a couple of days earlier so he could attend the last pool party of the year with me, but apparently the holiday weekend was super busy at the restaurant.

Besides the first date I'd missed, no Saturday ever went by where I didn't get to talk to him over dinner and share how my cooking skills were improving. Our relationship was continuing to grow, and he was even flirting with the idea of moving to Las Vegas. The restaurant he worked at already had a location out here, so it wouldn't be that hard to transition, but he wanted us to officially be together before committing to any big changes. I was hoping that he would finally ask me to be his girlfriend on his next visit.

I put on my newest bikini, figuring today would be a good day to try it out. Its gold and green tones were the same shade as Graham's eyes, and I was excited to show it off to him. However, I wanted to wear it once first, just in case it ended up not fitting right. With the way the mirror reflected how perfectly the suit hugged my body, I dismissed any such doubts. I knew Kyle would get a kick out of seeing me in it too.

I left the apartment, ready to attend the final Saturday party of the summer. Crazily enough, there was still a small part of me that always felt a sense of eagerness to see Kyle Kingsley every time I headed for the pool deck even though we had gone our separate ways after the dinner, but it was mostly because it was the only place we actually hung out. Our friendship was limited to the Exe Apartments, and I barely ever saw him anywhere else.

After the night he cooked me dinner, I'd thought there was going to be some sort of change in his behavior. He had realized that I was never going to give in to him so I tried rekindling a normal friendship, but it was really hard to build any type of relationship with him when we barely spoke. I tried texting him a few times to hang out, but he was always busy. I even offered to cook him dinner or buy him another pizza, but he was never willing to make time for me unless I was ready to finally remove my boundaries and give him what he truly wanted. I guess it was for the best, but I didn't like how our story concluded. We had known each other an entire summer, and Kyle still was not open to the idea of dating me. I knew I was going to end up choosing Graham in the end anyway, but it would've been nice for Kyle to at least make it a hard decision.

When I made it to the pool deck, Kyle smiled as he soaked in the view of me walking toward him in my new bikini. "Your body never ceases to amaze me," he exclaimed as I gave him a hug. "Too bad you're so stingy with it."

I was used to his suggestive comments by now, but was hoping that one day he'd find something else to compliment. He was always so flirty with me, and I never understood why he hadn't even been tempted to explore what we could've been. Graham was treating me the way I deserved to be treated, and I didn't have time to wait for Kyle to realize how great I was.

"The pool is closing tomorrow," I said, even though Kyle was clearly aware of this fact. "What's next for you?"

In a strange way, it was comforting to have him working at the Exe. I liked the consistency. He had been there ever since I moved in, and I couldn't help but reflect on how much our friendship had evolved. From drooling over him at a distance to going over to his house, we had been through a lot together, and nobody could deny that we had created a bond—even if it was unhealthy.

"I'm moving back to Sacramento," he told me. "My parents' life insurance money ran out, and without this job, I can't afford my apartment anymore."

Kyle's response crushed my heart. I'd been hoping he might get a different job at the apartment complex, but I'd known the possibility was low.

"I'm going to live with Eli and Mike. They are in town to help me move my stuff," he added.

As bipolar as his behavior had been throughout the summer, I wasn't ready for him to go. He didn't have to say it, but I knew that his move meant the end of our friendship.

"Are you going to get another job?" I asked. I selfishly hoped he wasn't going to be a pool security guard anywhere else. We both knew how hard it was for him to resist female attention.

"My brothers work at a car wash, so I'll probably just join them," he said casually.

It was sad knowing that Kyle was going to trade a low-income job in Nevada for another one in California. He didn't have the biggest career goals, but I hoped that one day he would eventually want more for himself.

"Well, give me one more hug just in case I don't see you again," I exclaimed, diving into his arms.

I savored his warm embrace, and the few tears that escaped my eyes were immediately soaked up by his shirt. It wasn't supposed to end like this. I wanted to remain in his arms for the rest of the day. I wasn't necessarily mourning the loss of Kyle, but I felt like I was losing a part of myself. I had poured so much of my emotions into him that I honestly didn't recognize myself anymore. So much of my energy that summer had been spent on Kyle, and I would have to watch all of my efforts just disappear. I wasn't ready to let him go. I didn't want to face the reality that I'd let another guy treat me in a way I shouldn't have accepted.

Being that it was the last pool party of the year, there was a long line of guests behind me that needed to be checked in. They were getting more impatient with each second that ticked by, so I released my hold on Kyle and let him proceed with his job. I entered the party wondering how I could possibly enjoy the day knowing that he was going to be gone tomorrow.

"Avery," Kyle called after me. "This won't be the last time you see me."

I turned and saw the sincerity in his expression. This was his final attempt at trying to strengthen the hold he had on me before we went our separate ways. I held his words close to my heart, knowing that they were going to be the only things to get me through his absence.

25
Opportunity Knocks

"I normally wouldn't complain about you cleaning the entire apartment, but it's been five hours, Avery," Paige griped as she watched me wipe down the kitchen counter for the hundredth time. "He doesn't even land until tomorrow afternoon."

I had spent the entire day preparing for Graham's arrival. It had been about a month since I last saw him, and I couldn't take the anticipation any longer. Our apartment hadn't even been that dirty to begin with, but I found cleaning to be the only activity that calmed my nerves. I was so eager to see him that I'd utilized a full bottle of disinfectant within the first hour. Every inch of the place was spotless, and the pantry was filled with Graham's favorite snacks. I'd also stocked the fridge with fresh ingredients for us to cook dinner with. He had sent me numerous recipes, and I was looking forward to trying them out with him.

"Where is he going to sleep?" Hannah innocently asked, joining Paige in her judgment of my excessive cleaning.

Paige and I exchanged timid glances. We hadn't talked about the sleeping arrangements, and we hadn't intended on discussing it either. It was a topic that neither of us were eager to explore. During his last visit, Graham had slept on the couch, but obviously things had changed since then. We were both probably hoping he would make the decision for us.

"Maybe you could sleep over at my place?" Hannah eagerly suggested to Paige after sensing the awkwardness.

She was never short of great ideas, and I was secretly hoping Paige would accept her offer. Obviously, I wanted Graham to be able to spend time with his sister too. I wasn't ignorant of the special bond they shared, but until Graham fully decided to move out here, our time together was limited, and Paige had spent her entire life with him.

"I guess I could stay over a few nights," she reluctantly agreed.

I hid my obnoxious grin behind a bottle of wipes and had an internal celebration as I shifted my cleaning efforts to the kitchen table.

The duration of Graham's trip was only four days, and he was going to spend some of it working at the steakhouse where we'd had our first date. The Vegas location would be his main base if he decided to move out here, so he wanted to get a feel for what it would be like. He also had a few apartment tours scheduled during his visit, which included one at the Exe. I offered to show him around myself, but he didn't think I was capable of giving him an unbiased tour. It was a great apartment complex, but I would definitely have overhyped the pool parties and exaggerated the half-priced appetizers. I didn't want to get my hopes up, but it seemed like a real possibility that Graham would adjust his entire life to be closer to me.

"I think you missed a spot," Paige joked as I continuously wiped down the same area of the table.

"Maybe she's planning on having a wild night while you're at my place," Hannah suggested.

"What happens in Vegas stays in Vegas." I winked.

Hannah and I almost died laughing, but Paige didn't find it very funny. I don't think she was too keen on imagining potential intimate moments between her best friend and her brother.

"I can't believe you even find him attractive," she said. "He literally looks like a lumberjack." Paige started shaking her head in disgust as if picturing him. Graham was not the most clean-shaven man I had ever met, but he definitely did not resemble a lumberjack.

"I thought we had a deal that if I watched the Thompsons for you, you wouldn't make fun of our relationship anymore," I casually reminded her.

Babysitting Riley and Wyatt hadn't been as bad as I thought it was going to be, but I had still held up my end of the deal, so I expected Paige to do the same.

"Ugh, you're right," she admitted in defeat.

I appreciated her promise to refrain from making more comments about Graham and me, but I wasn't convinced that this was going to be the last time.

"Hannah and I are actually about to head over to the Thompsons' house if you want to join us," Paige offered. "It's going to be Hannah's first time on an overnight gig."

The look on Hannah's face was a perfect mixture of excitement and fear. She was really enjoying her new career path, but sleeping over was a whole new venture. I had only spent a few hours at the Thompsons', and I'd been ready to pull my hair out by the time the parents returned. At least Paige was going to be there to support her.

"Sorry, I can't," I responded. "I've gotta get the apartment ready for Graham."

I finally concluded that the cleanliness of the kitchen met my standards and shifted my focus to the living room. Paige rolled her eyes, since she knew this would be my third time organizing the area today, but she and Hannah had already managed to create a mess since the last time I'd cleaned.

"Alright, Cinderella," Paige said, "but don't let your fairy godmother turn your car into a pumpkin, or Graham is going to have to walk to our apartment from the airport."

The sound of the vacuum drowned out the rest of her comments. For her sake, I was glad she was going to be spending some nights at Hannah's, because I was planning on shedding a lot more than just a glass slipper.

The quietness that flooded the apartment when Paige and Hannah left for the Thompsons' created the perfect environment for me to call it an early night, but my excitement about seeing Graham kept me awake. Even spending the entire day scrubbing every inch of the apartment hadn't been enough to exhaust me. I was able to eventually close my eyes, but I never fell into a deep sleep. I could not stop thinking about Graham long enough to fully relax. The slightest noise would wake me up, so I wasn't surprised when I was alert enough to hear the front door crack open at four in the morning. I figured Paige had forgotten something or Hannah had tapped out of the overnight babysitting. Based on my one experience at the Thompsons', my money was on Hannah. Riley was a handful, and I didn't think I would've been able to spend an entire night, let alone the next morning, with her.

Hannah had been to our apartment numerous times, so I was surprised by the amount of noise she was making. It sounded like she was searching for something, but I could tell she hadn't turned the living room lights on. She probably assumed I was asleep and didn't want to wake me, but the sounds of her stumbling over the furniture in the dark was more disruptive than turning on the lamp and grabbing whatever she'd left behind would have been.

I waited a few more minutes, but the rustling continued. Drawers were being opened, papers were being shuffled through, and the amount of activity made me believe that there was more than one person in the apartment. The noises continued to echo from the kitchen, and I almost left my room to see what was going on, but the fear of not knowing what lay on the other side of my door kept me bound to my bed. Maybe it really was Hannah and Paige looking for something. They weren't the most responsible human beings on the planet when it came to keeping track of things.

My nerves paralyzed me even further when I heard the sounds move to Paige's room. Based on all the movement on the other side of the wall, I could tell her stuff was being rummaged through. I was still holding on to the hope that it was Hannah and Paige I was hearing, but I realized things could take a serious turn for the worse if I was wrong.

For a split second, I swallowed my fear and decided that the best thing for me to do was to sneak out the back door of my room. If my friends were truly the ones here, we would be able to look back and laugh at this. However, all the commotion made me highly doubt it. I needed to lock my bedroom door first, because the sound of the heavy sliding door would alarm whoever was in the apartment, and they would run into my room.

I quietly slipped out of bed. The hardwood floors creaked every time I shifted my weight from one floorboard to another. I tried to slow my steps in an effort not to startle the intruders, but my heavy feet made it obvious that they were not alone. The rustling in Paige's room had come to a sudden halt and was replaced by footsteps heading in my direction. I ditched my initial idea of being quiet and decided to make a run for it. I lunged for the door, but the darkness disoriented me, and I miscalculated my surroundings. Instead of reaching the lock, I drove my pinky toe into the corner of my desk and fell to the ground with a loud thud. The faint footsteps I had heard earlier turned into a thunderous stampede as they quickly approached my room.

I tried to recover from my fall, but only managed to stand up in time to see the twist of the doorknob. Paige and Hannah were clearly not the ones I had heard, because standing in the doorway were three large men dressed in black. Their faces were covered by ski masks, so I couldn't tell who they were, even though the darkness would've made that impossible anyway.

My pinky toe was throbbing, but my fight-or-flight instincts kicked in, and without wasting another second, I turned my back to the men and ran for the back door. My mission was unsuccessful, and I was only able to pull back the curtains before a hand covered in a black glove wrapped itself around my neck. It continued to squeeze the breath out of me as I struggled for air. I tried to put up a fight, but it made no difference.

The moonlight shone in through the back door, illuminating a small portion of my room. At least my last moments weren't going to take place in complete darkness. I'd have one last chance to see the effervescent moon staring back at me as my life slowly slipped away. I used the last burst of strength I had left at another attempt to try to free myself, but the intruder's grip only tightened. The evil serpent inked into his skin was the last image I saw before the world around me went black.

26
Home Is Where the Exe Is

I had never been able to watch scary movies before bed without having nightmares. One time, a character drowned in the final scene, and that night I found myself in a dream where my foot was anchored to the bottom of the deepest depths of the ocean. I woke up gasping for air and soaking in a pool of my own sweat. It was one of the worst night terrors I ever had.

When I awoke to find myself tied to my desk chair, I hoped that it was just another dream inspired by some crime show I'd fallen asleep watching. Unfortunately, I vividly remembered turning on a romantic comedy after I finished cleaning. The pain around my neck and the restraints around my wrists and ankles were very real.

The three men who'd entered my apartment were standing around in a circle, clearly unhappy with one another. From the way the sun was barely peeking into my room, I guessed it was around six in the morning. Still too early for Paige or Hannah to return from the Thompsons', and definitely too early for Graham to have landed and realized something was wrong when I wasn't there to pick him up. I wished he had taken the morning flight.

The dim light revealed that the intruders had ransacked my entire room. They'd searched through all of my drawers and left behind a disastrous mess. I twisted my wrists and ankles, testing the tightness of the ropes around them. My struggle alarmed the men and forced a sudden pause in their argument.

"What are we supposed to do with her?" a deep voice demanded.

I almost recognized the voice, but it was his authoritative demeanor that gave him away. His dominant presence and bossiness were the true essence of his personality. It came with being the eldest sibling. From the way he was hovering around the two other men, I could tell that Eli Kingsley was frustrated with the situation he and his brothers found themselves in.

"This wasn't my idea." The voice sounded like it belonged to Mike Kingsley. "I'm just doing what I was told."

The two brothers went back and forth before finally facing Kyle. Despite both of them being older, they were evidently under his influence. Perhaps he wasn't speaking because he knew I would recognize his voice, but his tattoo had already given him away. He remained suspiciously calm and seemed unfazed by his brothers' worries. Carefully walking over, he knelt down so that he was eye-level with me. He slowly removed his ski mask and stared straight into my soul.

"Where's the money, Avery?" Kyle calmly whispered. He ran his fingers over my thighs and flashed his usual smile at me.

"What are you talking about?" I frantically stammered. "What money?"

I struggled against the ropes that held me in place. My new salary had afforded me the ability to carry a higher balance in my bank account, but I doubted that was what he was referring to.

Kyle stood up and made his way over to the back of the chair. He took his gloved hand and wrapped his fingers around my neck. "We can do this the easy way or the hard way." He began to tighten his grip as I gasped for air. "Now, we both know you prefer a little choking, but I promise not to hurt you if you just give me what I want."

He continued to squeeze until I started to fade in and out of consciousness. Kyle released his grip just before the world went black again. He let me recover before returning to view and continuing his line of questioning.

"Tell us where the money is, Avery," he demanded.

"I don't know what you're talking about," I managed to croak once I'd regained my breath.

Kyle was growing more and more irritated. He started pacing back and forth across the room, grabbing the back of his neck like he usually did when he was nervous. I was in a lot of pain, but was distracted by my growing sense of confusion. What money was he referring to, and why was he so sure that I was in possession of it?

His frustration became contagious, and Eli grew increasingly annoyed, deciding to join Kyle in his pacing. He started walking in circles until his anger eventually took over. Eli walked straight over to me and punched me directly in the mouth. Splatters of blood began staining my carpet as he continued to destroy my face.

"Get off her!" Kyle screamed, pulling his brother away from me.

He began taking shots at Eli's jaw until Mike eventually separated them. The whole scene was chaotic, and whatever their plan was, it was clearly falling apart.

"I thought you said she was rich," Mike eventually said.

"She is," Kyle assured him breathlessly. "Her dad left her an envelope here somewhere. There's $25,000 in it. We just gotta find it."

I'd always known lying was bad, but I never thought it would cause three crazy men to break into my apartment, tie me to a chair, and demand money. It wasn't that hard to get into my unit considering it was always unlocked, and Kyle had access to the building since he worked here, but I still hadn't expected it. When I'd lied to Kyle and said my dad had given me the money, I was too embarrassed to admit that he'd actually gambled the last of his lottery winnings away. I had been trying to impress Kyle, but all it did was land me in a dangerous situation. It had never crossed my mind that he would try to rob me. Eli had severely damaged my face, but Kyle's betrayal was the ultimate gut punch.

Kyle went to my bathroom to fetch a few tissues. He started dabbing the blood from the corners of my mouth and tucked my hair behind my ears.

"Nobody touches her except me," he growled.

He discarded the tissue and positioned himself so that his lips were directly against my ear. "Now listen, Avery," he began as he stroked my hair. "You and I have some unfinished business, don't we?"

Kyle moved his mouth even closer and started nibbling on my earlobe. The sensation sent chills through my body. "I believe last time we were rudely interrupted by the fire alarm," he reminded me as he continued to kiss my ear. "And the time before that, I believe you accidentally got a little too excited." He started massaging the leg that had kicked him in the stomach. "You didn't mean it though, did you, Avery?"

I hesitantly shook my head.

"Now I know you like to entertain people, but I was hoping our first time together would be a little more . . . private." He was now flicking his tongue against my ear. The wetness against my skin made me shudder.

"So you can either tell me where the envelope is, or"—Kyle turned to face Eli and Mike before finishing—"we are going to give my brothers a little show." He tugged at the hem of my shirt.

Kyle had always been my weakness, tempting me into succumbing to his ways. When I wanted a relationship, he'd tried to lure me into a casual fling. When I tried to build an emotional connection with him, he'd tried to entice me to engage in the physical side of things. The only time Kyle had even slightly let his guard down was when I'd given in to his desires. The more I struggled against his seductions, the more he would continue to entice me, but if I showed small signs of surrender, he would alleviate some of the pressure. I was hoping that this still remained true, since I wasn't sure how else I was going to escape this nightmare.

"I think we should give them a little show," I answered, a string of bloody drool hanging from my lip.

Kyle stumbled over his breath. As much as he'd been dying to get a free pass at my body, the cash was way more important to him.

"Just tell us where the money is and this will all be over," Mike pleaded.

He seemed to want the whole situation to end almost as much as I did. The way he was shaking in his shoes made me fearful that the bloodstains on my carpet were going to be joined by his urine.

Eli stormed over to me as if he was going to damage the small portion of my face that had managed to escape his attack the first time, but Kyle held him back.

"If she's not going to talk on her own, at least let me force it out of her," Eli insisted.

He proceeded to wind up his fist, but Kyle stood firm in his stance. "If you touch her, I'll kill you," he hissed.

"Oh, you mean just like how you killed Mom and Dad?" Eli fired back.

This revelation was not only shocking to me, but appeared to take Mike by surprise as well. I watched him lean against the wall to prevent himself from falling over.

"You killed them?" Mike shouted in despair. He started dry heaving and grasping at his chest. I was afraid he was going to pass out.

"You weren't complaining when I gave you your portion of the life insurance money," Kyle snapped back at Eli.

"My portion?" his brother said. "How much was your portion?"

"Well, I did all the hard work," Kyle countered, clearly regretting mentioning the money.

"That's it," Eli concluded. "I'm out of here." He stormed out of the room, dragging Mike with him.

"What about the cops?" Mike asked cautiously, trailing behind.

"We have masks on, you idiot," Eli returned. "She doesn't know who we are."

Out of the three of them, Eli's intelligence was the most questionable. It didn't take a genius to identify them, especially after they'd just admitted to having the same parents as Kyle.

"What about Kyle?" Mike helplessly pointed out.

Kyle had removed his mask a while ago and didn't seem worried that his identity had been revealed. "Don't worry," he asserted. "She won't snitch on me." He caressed my cheek and kissed my bruised forehead. "We have been through too much together."

He got into position behind me and arranged his hand around my neck as he had done earlier. This time, I didn't struggle as my vision began to blur and my lungs started to panic. I welcomed unconsciousness and was hoping it would find me sooner rather than later.

"This won't be the last time you see me, Avery," Kyle whispered in my ear.

And then suddenly, the world around me disappeared.

27
Enough

Apparently, Hannah had tapped out of the babysitting gig early and returned to our apartment to retrieve some of her belongings an hour or so after the Kingsley brothers had left. She wasted no time in calling the cops as soon as she found my unconscious body still tied to my desk chair. My face was bruised pretty badly, and there were marks around my neck, wrists, and ankles, but I think my spirit had taken the hardest hit. I had put my trust in someone who'd ended up stabbing me in the back. Kyle hadn't taken any money, but he'd robbed me of my innocence.

I was eager to see Paige and Hannah after the traumatic incident, but the police wouldn't let anyone into my hospital room until they'd finished their questioning. Needless to say, Kyle was right regarding my lack of inclination to snitch on him. The detective spent hours interrogating me and asking me the same questions over and over, just slightly rephrased, hoping I would give him additional information. The only details I was willing to provide was that they'd hid their identities and that there had been three of them. I didn't even give away their body types or heights, claiming it had been too dark to make an accurate assessment.

I wasn't necessarily trying to protect the Kingsley brothers, especially after discovering the truth about what had happened to their parents, but Kyle was right. We had been through a lot together during the short time we'd known each other. I knew he had a troubled past, and I didn't want to add to it. Despite being hesitant to let people get close to him, Kyle had allowed me into his life, and I didn't want to punish him for that. I hadn't turned my back on him yet, and I didn't want to start. I didn't plan on speaking to him again anyway, so I figured it was best to just peacefully go our separate ways.

"Alright, well, if you remember anything else," the detective said as he handed me his business card, "please don't hesitate to reach out."

I smiled and nodded, eager for him to leave so that Paige and Hannah could come in. Instead, nurses flooded the room to conduct a few more tests before they would allow any guests. One of them took a cotton swab and attempted to brush the area around my ear with it.

"What are you doing?" I yelled as I jerked my body away from her.

"You have slight discoloration in the area, miss," the nurse informed me, pointing to where Kyle had nibbled my ear.

"I wasn't strangled there," I snapped at her. "I was choked at the base of my neck." I pointed to the place where Kyle had wrapped his hand around me.

"This abrasion appears to resemble a bite mark," the nurse said politely. "Your attackers wore gloves, so unfortunately, we were not able to identify any fingerprints. I'm trying to see if we can collect DNA evidence if saliva was left behind."

I didn't even let her finish before I slapped the cotton swab out of her hand. I hit it so hard that it flung across the room and landed underneath a chair. Her face dropped.

"Leave my ear alone," I growled as she took a few steps away from me.

The other nurses stared at me in fear.

"Let's just give her a break," one of them eventually said. "Her boyfriend is here. He's in the waiting room and has been asking to see her."

Graham. I hadn't realized how long I had been in the hospital. He'd probably freaked out when he landed and heard what happened to me.

"Can I see him?" I asked calmly, hoping that my recent act wouldn't hinder my ability to have visitors.

"Absolutely," one of the nurses told me.

My room was quickly emptied out to allow space for the people who had been waiting patiently for me in the lobby. Hannah, with her fiery red curls, entered first. I immediately teared up at the sight of her, wondering how much worse shape I would've ended up in if she hadn't returned to the apartment early. Paige followed closely behind and ran over to give me a hug as soon as she saw me. Hannah joined in, and the three of us embraced in a bawling mess.

"I'm so sorry," Paige choked out through a sea of tears. "I'll never forget to lock the door again."

I hugged her tighter, signaling that I forgave her. It wasn't her fault that Kyle and his brothers decided to break into our apartment.

"I brought you a present, but I'm not sure if you'll like it."

Paige sniffled as she made her way over to the door. Before she'd even opened it fully, Graham rushed in and wrapped his arms around me. The last time I'd seen him cry was when he was heartbroken over Sarah, but there were definitely a few tears escaping his eyes now.

"The first time I flew out here, you rammed your chair into me," he said, fighting back tears, "and this time, I find out that you've been attacked." He squeezed me a little tighter as Hannah and Paige retreated to the back of the room to give us some space.

"I guess you're just going to have to move out here," I declared as I held him in my arms.

"I heard the Exe has a few vacancies," he said, pulling my face in for a warm kiss. The bruises around my mouth throbbed at the sudden contact, but it was definitely worth it.

"Get a room!" Paige shouted from the corner.

"We had a deal!" I fired back with a smile as I removed one of the pillows from my bed and threw it at her. I didn't think Paige was ever going to stop commenting on my relationship with Graham, but in that moment, that was the last thing on my mind.

We were interrupted by a gentle knock on the door. The nurse whose cotton swab I'd assaulted peeked her head into the room. "Avery," she began, "your parents are here."

I looked at Paige, but she gently shook her head, indicating that she was not the one who had notified them. Hannah wasn't even in possession of their contact information, so I knew it couldn't have been her. I turned my attention to Graham, who had a look of guilt across his face.

"They were staying at a motel close by," he timidly explained. "I figured they deserved to know what happened to their daughter."

The room fell silent.

"Well, she's definitely not going to date you now," Paige grumbled. She and Graham went back and forth in their usual sibling banter until the nurse eventually interrupted them.

"Should I have them leave?" she asked in my direction. I had already slapped a cotton swab out of her hand, so I didn't think she wanted to give me any other reason to get angry.

My parents were honestly the last people I wanted to see. I was surprised that they hadn't returned back to Michigan, but I supposed that would have required money. It was weird knowing that they had been living in the same city as me this whole time. I'd never planned on seeing them again, but feeling my life be slowly drained from me by a guy I'd trusted had put things into a whole new perspective.

"You can let them in," I said nervously.

Hannah, Paige, and Graham left to give me some alone time with my parents. Paige offered to stay behind, but I assured her that everything would be okay. A few moments after everyone had cleared the room, the nurse returned with my mother and father. They had aged a lot more than they should've in the past couple of months. Their clothes were dirty and torn, and their skin was blotted with dirt. I wouldn't have been surprised if they were actually living on the streets of Vegas rather than a motel. They sure smelled like it.

"How are you feeling?" my mother inquired as she approached my bed.

"I'm fine, Mom," I answered.

My parents came and stood by my bedside, and an awkward silence fell. We felt more like strangers than family.

"We got here as soon as Graham called us," my dad informed.

Graham and my father used to golf together before Dad won the lottery. We'd lived near a course, so as soon as the weather was appropriate, they would find themselves out playing. Since my dad never turned down an opportunity to gamble, he often put a wager on their rounds. From the way he would return home upset, I knew Graham had won most of the bets.

"He cares a lot about you," my mom interjected. She looked relieved knowing that there was someone in my life to look after me when they had failed to do that very thing.

"Graham is a good guy," I confirmed.

It was weird having a talk about a boy with her so soon after she'd reappeared into my life. I wondered if this was how Paige's catch-up calls with her mom went.

"Do you think you could ever forgive us?" my mother desperately asked. "Your father and I are really sorry about not being there for you."

I'd always dreamed of the day when my parents would stop traveling the world so that we could be a family again. It used to be one of my biggest desires in life. Their apology was a step in the right direction, but it would take a lot more than that for me to forgive them, and a whole lot more to feel like their daughter again.

"Maybe one day," I told her.

It was as truthful an answer as I could give them in that moment. I wasn't sure what the future held, but I knew I wasn't ready to fully shut my parents out if they were willing to change. It felt like our relationship was at rock bottom, so at least we could only go up from here.

It was nice to have this private moment with my parents, but I was very relieved when Paige, Hannah, and Graham came back into the room. Graham was even carrying a fresh bouquet of roses. He was no stranger to buying me flowers, but I think he was partially motivated by trying to make a good impression on my parents. I took the bouquet from him and inhaled the lovely aroma.

"He calls himself your 'Graham cracker'?" my mom asked. There was a card attached to the flowers, but I must have knocked it off when I'd taken them from him. I quickly snatched it from her and read it for myself.

I'd love to officially be the Graham cracker to your s'mores. Will you be my girlfriend?

A tear welled up in the corner of my eye, but I quickly wiped it away and reached for Graham's hand. I pulled him close to me and nodded passionately.

"And I'd love to be the chocolate to yours," I said, blushing.

"Now all we need is a marshmallow," Graham whispered as he pulled me in for a kiss.

I wasn't sure how my day had started as my worst nightmare and ended as my wildest dream, but I was happy to be surrounded by my favorite people. Hannah had rescued me from my apartment, Paige had helped me find myself, and Graham had restored my faith in love. I hadn't known how my life was going to end up when I left Michigan to start over in Nevada, but I never could have envisioned this. There were lots of bumps along the way, and I even lost myself during parts of the journey, but at the end of the day, I was where I was supposed to be.

I didn't regret any of my decisions, because they'd led me to this moment, but I'd learned to be more careful in who I let into my life. The treatment that I accepted was a direct reflection of what I thought of myself. I didn't believe I was pretty enough or good enough to be with the kind of guy I'd thought existed only in movies or my dreams. Who was I to think that I could end up with someone who bought me flowers or actually cared about my feelings? I'd viewed myself as unworthy, so I let an unworthy guy mistreat me. I gave in to his temptations and strayed even further away from the life that I truly wanted to live. It had taken a tragic incident for me to get back on the right path, but I had a lot of great company to help me along the way. I wasn't sure what the rest of my life had in store, but I was excited to experience it with this new mindset. I was enough, and I would always be enough.

28
They Always Come Back

"They always come back," Paige reassured Hannah as Leo, Toby, Benny, and Tubs ran out through the back door of the apartment to explore the Vegas landscape.

Paige carried a pile of boxes into the kitchen and set them down on the table. A thick layer of duct tape was wrapped around them, making it appear as though they weren't meant to be opened.

"What's inside those boxes?" I asked.

Hannah's interest was also piqued, and she joined me at the kitchen table.

"Money, disguises, and fake passports . . ." Paige announced, followed by loud laughter as she watched the alarmed reactions on Hannah's and my faces, "just in case we need to disappear for a while . . . or make someone disappear for a while."

She winked at me as she carried the load of boxes to her room. The way Paige chuckled made it seem as though she were joking, but something told me her answer wasn't a total lie.

It had been about a year since I was attacked by the Kingsley brothers, and a lot had changed. Once our lease was up, Paige and I moved into a three-bedroom unit and added Hannah as our third roommate. We kept our location on the ground floor so the cats could roam, but Hannah wasn't too thrilled about the idea of Tubs aimlessly walking around the perimeter of the Exe. Paige swore that the cats would always return, and so far, they always had.

Graham stayed true to his word and ended up moving to Vegas a few months after the incident. He served as the head chef at his restaurant's Vegas location and even named a fleet of appetizers "The Avery," inspired by our first date. Despite the delicious assortment of small plates, it was the filet mignon that eventually won him numerous awards and made his restaurant a Las Vegas staple. Celebrities from all over the world traveled to try his famously cooked steak. My cooking skills were nowhere near as good as Graham's, but they had improved drastically from when we'd first started dating. I was more cut out for social media anyway, which worked out perfectly when I quit my job at Ace Modeling Agency to be the chief marketing officer for Graham's restaurant.

Graham toured several apartments before deciding to also move into the Exe. He insisted that the other places were not up to his standard, but secretly, he probably just wanted to be close enough to keep an eye on Paige and me. Paige didn't seem to mind that her brother lived in the same complex, but that was probably because she was barely even home. She'd decided to start her own caretaking business that connected wealthy families with highly rated nannies. Hannah was one of the nannies in the network, and it kept them both very busy.

Between the amount of time Paige and Hannah spent babysitting and the amount of time I spent at Graham's apartment, our unit was usually vacant. Paige had learned her lesson regarding locking doors, though, so despite our place being a great target for another robbery, it was always tightly secured.

My growing relationship with my parents posed its normal challenges. My mother missed traveling the world and would often fall into a depressed state and not want to talk to anyone. She canceled a lot of plans with me because of her saddened mood, but when Paige's mom was able to land her a job as a travel agent, these episodes became far less frequent.

The surrounding temptation to gamble constantly tugged at my father's heart. He found himself in casinos more times than he should've, but at least he only played with the profit he was earning from his new job, which wasn't that much. Because of his love for money, he'd tried to build a career in finance, but his rocky past had put a strain on that dream. Instead, he landed a job as a cashier at a local grocery store. He was handling money, but not in the way he wanted to. My relationship with my parents was ever evolving, but at least they were trying, and that was all I could ask for.

With our busy lives, Paige, Hannah, and I rarely attended the Saturday pool parties anymore. When we did show up, we noticed that the Exe had hired a new security guard. He appeared to be in his early thirties and looked like a former military officer. I was over my days of flirting with the apartment employees, but apparently older Army men were exactly Hannah's type. Paige and I were extremely apprehensive about our friend's new love interest, especially because of what had happened to me, but after watching them go on several dates and observing his love for cats, we were very supportive when she came home one night engaged. It seemed not all pool security guards were awful.

I never saw Kyle again, but I was pretty sure he was somewhere out in the world luring another girl into his seductive trap. At least it wasn't me this time. The last memory I had of him was him telling me that this wouldn't be the last time I saw him as he began to suffocate me. Fortunately, that was a threat he hadn't followed through on. It had been almost a year, and I hadn't heard a single word from him. I wasn't planning on seeing him anytime soon, but for some reason, I wasn't totally convinced I was never going to hear from him again. Besides . . . they always come back.

About The Author

Thank you for reading my first self-published book, *They Always Come Back*. It took a lot of courage for me to step outside of my comfort zone and write from the depths of my imagination. I've spent a lot of time reading romance novels and always envisioned writing my own one day. With a little bit of creativity and a lot of help, I was able to bring my wildest fantasies to life.

I encourage you to share this book with a friend who might be in need of an entertaining love story and to sign up for my newsletter for updates regarding upcoming releases. I appreciate your love and support as I continue my writing journey.

Subscribe to my newsletter:
https://linktr.ee/authorbaileythomas

Printed in Great Britain
by Amazon